KEVIN COYNE

THAT OLD SUBURBAN ANGST

www.kevincoynebooks.com

This Edition Published 2004
By Tony Donaghey Publishing - England
For
www.kevincoynebooks.com

ISBN 0-9549003-0-8

Copyright: Kevin Coyne 2004

This book is sold subject to the condition that it shall not by way of trade or otherwise, be lent, hired out, or otherwise circulated without the publisher's prior consent in any form of binding or cover other than that in which it is published and without a similar condition including this condition being imposed on the subsequent purchaser.

Printed and Bound by
The Charlesworth Group Wakefield

CONTENTS

That Old Suburban Angst	1
Thin Walls	2
A Chat With My Darling	4
Aids	5
Life Stories	8
Rabbit Teeth	33
How He Is	38
Lady Luck	39
Rat Head	39
On The River Bank	40
A Little Love Story	41
A Writer's Lot	42
Getting Better	43
Dark Into Light	44
A Perfect Sunday	45
Love Story	46
To A Sibling	47
Heads	48
Encyclopaedia A.B.C.D	51
- Albania	52
- Angst	52
- Paul Anka	52
- Anorexia	53
- Arab	54
- Adolf	55
- Bavaria	56
- British	56
- Bananas	58
- Bride	60
- Bastard	60
- Beans	62
- Cholera	64
- Christ	64
- Couch	66
- Coventry	66
- Computer	67
- Cousin	68
- Diarrhoea	69
- Diploma	71
- Doctor	71
- Diamonds	72
- Denmark	73
- Dynamite	74
Jim and Lydia Chew The Fat	75
Junior	79
Parrot	82
Psychosis In The Sunshine	85
Taciturn Tompkins	90
Topsy Turvy Time	94
Alan's Search For True Love	110
Occurrences	116
A True Friend	130
Alive	132
Days By The Sea	135
With Maria By The Sea	137
My Life With Ronald and Others	139
Liverpool Arthur	143

THAT OLD SUBURBAN ANGST

It's hard to tell you how I feel because all feeling was almost forgotten the day I dropped my trousers in the town centre.
Oh the shitty shame it caused, the rollicking laughter that ensued from the gobs of all present. Martin, mixed up missile of a mouse thing from nowhere, was no help at all.
"Fallollock," he shouted (a new word he'd invented for the occasion) "Fallollock." But trousers were lost, buttocks got free, police called to witness and finally punish. I spent two weeks in an open prison near Biggleswade. "Next time we'll put you in with the proper perverts," said the officer in charge the day before my sentence ended, "with all the kinky dross from this aching arsehole of a universe." Then my heart went bumpabumpabumpa while the dragon of misfortune clawed meaningfully down my archy starchy backbone. Ghostly church bells were tolling. At least six fat men invited me to bounce up and down with them in the prison vegetable garden.
Back home little Ernest had left Sarah Sausage and somebody had given my job at the florists to a chap with big ears. Oh those lost days when I stood outside my former place of work witnessing that usurper go about his business, watching him snip, snip, snip and stuffily preen. I came close to strangling the monstrosity on more than one occasion. His cockiness cocked me up almost permanently. I would have cut off his cock if I'd been curmudgeon enough. Unemployment doth not seek to edify or uplift. It's true that those without are made to feel more so. Martin, my atom-age friend, has often added much to the distinct lack of scrumptiousness in my life. "Footling," he's been heard to say after I've made a major statement about the whys and wherefores of life, "Footling and fartling and foolhardiness." Tears well up sometimes but I suppress them. My steely determination to remain untouched by cruel adversity is legendary in these parts.
And what has really become of that forthright, chubby, overly opinionated redhead, Sarah Sausage? There has been talk of a corpse in the woods, of a sack bag stuffed with body parts left outside Alf Crownson's garage. The police have denied all knowledge, choosing to fiddle faddle on about exhibitionists at bus stops and stolen underwear from suburban gardens.

Are we ever to find out the truth? Little Ernest claims to know nothing."She left me in the lurch outside Grabham's the butchers," is all he can splutter out when pressed. How achingly sad some situations are. Where are you Sarah Sausage? I'm twenty-eight years old and in grave need of love's wondrous spell. Didn't you once touch my backside one wet Christmas holiday outside your cousin's bungalow, and wasn't it I who expressed my gratitude by reaching out for your left breast? Oh why did you sway to avoid me? What was it about me that made you resist after such a promising start? Oh gossipy, bubbly, bouncy butterball of a thing, am I to be cast aside forever? I lust for you, you little know all. Come out from this shroud of darkness you knitted for yourself - present yourself before me! Little Edgar knows but isn't saying, titters to himself between shots of whiskey in our local while slowly drinking himself mad. His doleful story about being left high and dry outside Grabham's is a lie.

Rumour has it he was the jealous type, jealous enough to kill.

I've a good mind to question him closely next time he staggers into me in the bar, pull sharply at his earlobes, torture the truth out of him.

These are hard times we live in. What chance has a man who bared his arse in public and was imprisoned for it got in this poxy town?

A murder suspect like little Edgar gets more respect. Martin, my childhood wanking partner with a cruel knack for judging me harshly, showed a rare touch of compassion the other day when he counselled me to keep the old trousers on and "laugh at the clouds." The poetic lilt to his advice almost brought me to tears.

I'm surrounded by secretive people keeping secrets, small town nobodies with power complexes, sexually bombastic creatures championing open sex, rape and bestiality. Is it any wonder a man drops his trousers occasionally? The atmosphere in these parts is electric with lust and, if the truth be known, only adds to the potent whiff of raging desire that frequently engulfs me. My arse has to feel the sun, the snow, the whipping, snarling winter rains. I am a victim of a suburban angst.

THIN WALLS

Now the moon has gone and the neighbours click dominoes in the dark. Thin walls, all my life I've been a martyr to thin walls. We of the lower classes would love to be party to thicker walls but near poverty has condemned us to the thinner type. It's to do with expensive bricks and mortar. Those with lots of money can afford to splash out, make walls stout, and ensure they are secure. We without the wherewithal are forced to do with plaster board. Our opinions on housing and the like are very rarely asked for. Where's the justice, chamois leather purses, hands bedecked with fanciable rings? I'm barely employable. I can't afford anything. They were fighting next door last night. She was heard to hit him with a metal object of some sort, one that caused a shimmering cymbal like sound that gave me earache.

I meant to complain when I met them on the corridor this morning but was afraid. Last time I protested the male cuffed me round the back of my head, called me "Kenneth the Pipsqueak." I was humiliated to the point of becoming suicidal and buying a very sharp bread knife. Do you like sliced bread? I don't. I'm utterly browned off with both its consistency and its ability to stick in the throats of young children. "Oh no, he choked on the dough!" I heard a young mother scream once in the casualty ward of one of London's most famous hospitals.

A bread knife would come in handy. I should buy some proper curtains. Since she went off with the kids to Birkenhead I've had very little time to concentrate on practicals. My ambitions remain undiluted though. The life of a papal dignitary still interests me. She, quite naturally, didn't think much of the idea, often choosing to make funny faces behind my back if I so much as mentioned the topic. Little did she know that I frequently caught her at it in my shaving mirror. I wonder why she always did it when were standing in the bathroom together? The few times she got down on her knees to lower my underpants to my ankles with her teeth were interesting. Our last two years together were shit. Being alone isn't the epiphany to divine silence I expected it to be. Thin walls lead to noise. Ghosts, I've found, find them easier to travel through. First there was Dennis Wooley, a former school chum, who emerged a month ago to lecture me about my unwashed duvet, boldly suggesting that I was "turning into a tramp" and "wasn't worth a twopenny toss." I took offence of course, but couldn't kick him in the balls because the elusive nature of his transparent state. Ghosts are arrogant, quarrelsome, over familiar (they talk as if they know everything about you) troublemakers. Take the eternally petite Linda Wantage, for instance. What a saucy bit of cosmic fluff! She once danced wide-eyed and nearly naked on the end of my bed, then proceeded to call me "a dirty-minded voyeur" afterwards for, "staring all the time." It was all so frustratingly illogical. Her sexual teasing succeeded, although she denied me my pleasure by spreading guilt. Thin walls lead to truculent female ghosts imposing themselves on men. I must somehow persuade my landlord to make them thicker, perhaps to forget the costs and consider the sanity of one of his tenants. I've been left high and dry by a woman without a heart. My two sons (still so young!) have probably forgotten me by now. My kind are made for crouching dumbfounded in quiet corners, stuffing themselves with stale sandwiches from rubbish bins in railway station waiting rooms, belching to amuse themselves in artic Salvation Army dormitories. The next time my neighbours pass me in the hall they'll more than likely wrestle me to the floor. It's to be expected. They have the upper hand. I'm the one that creeps round his flat in socks to avoid making excess noise when they're at their dominoes and gin rummy. I'm the one that shakes their doormat every weekend because the female of the house has an allergy to dust. I'm just mouse droppings. The rats will chew through my exceedingly thin walls soon, making sure they sing me a happy song as they jangle on their banjos. They could eat my feet off. Its been done before. My brother in Derby suffered this fate a few years ago.

A CHAT WITH MY DARLING

Darling, at your next junket could you wear my underpants on your head? It makes sense. We that are rich are rich because we've invariably taken ourselves too seriously. Let's surprise the world with our barefaced cheek. If I wear those transparent panties of yours and stuff an ostrich feather up my arse the result could be a sensation. We'd be the gossip topic of the village. Julie Smallwood would have to take notice. Your rejection by the ladies bridge team would suddenly be seen as an oversight to be rectified immediately. Petty little Smallwood would probably lose her captain's badge. This rotten society that's ignored us for so long will perhaps truly embrace us for the first time. The prospect of all this occurring causes itching. I can't sit still for long. How strange it is to be as sensitive as I. The Baldrians, our standoffish neighbours with the pack of you yapping Highland terriers, shouted cruel but difficult to hear insults across the topiary yesterday. I started breaking wind loudly because of it. My summer shorts billowed out alarmingly. Thank God I didn't itch though. Any irritation in the summer heat could have caused insects to settle on my person, perhaps devour bits of me. I've seen photographs of victims of this in a magazine, poor raddled fools with torment in their eyes. God does not intend I go through this kind of ordeal. Darling, a heavenly sort of place is his eventual intention for both of us. I have heard this in my prayers.

AIDS

Carol says she's got AIDS, broadcasts it all over the public bar most evenings. "AIDS," she'll say. "Fuckin` AIDS at my tender age." My mate Ronnie thinks its all fantasy, that she's never had a sexual encounter in her life. I'm not so sure myself. I've heard stories of her fiddling and fooling with any bloke willing to take a chance. Life at our university can get a bit wild at times. AIDS could be everywhere couldn't it? Both my parents gave me a stern warning before term started. Dad talked about "the old cages of Bombay" and "women with welcoming smiles bearing sexual lust in their hearts." I pretended to be concerned. Mother noticed and burst out laughing. "Old soldiers are all the same", she said, gently refusing to elaborate further. Ronnie got the same treatment from his folks. His mother demanded she be called every evening and given a full report of the days affairs, claiming she was worried out of her mind by the promiscuity on campus. Life's weird sometimes. My pal Ronnie always undresses in the dark whereas I like to flaunt my wedding tackle whenever I get the chance. Is it wrong to be proud of what I've got? Ronnie always looks so pissed off when I do it. Carol called him "a dickless wonder" two weeks ago just because he wouldn't drop his trousers in the pub car park for a bet. His face went all red when she said it. I felt a bit sorry for him. He's obviously as sensitive as hell about his privates. Another friend of mine, the incorrigible Ian Partington, likes fox hunting, rides off with the hounds two or three times a year. Carol frequently tells him off about it. "I'd rather have AIDS than bloodlust," she's often heard to say. I think it's all a bit bloody ironic. The poor girl's got her values wrong. I'm planning to go into psychiatry when I graduate. Ronnie fancies the idea of becoming a famous landscape gardener. Ian Partington, forever the rebel amongst us, talks jokingly of becoming "a dustman to the rich" when he graduates. And Carol. What's her future for Christ's sake? I prefer to look on the bright side and assume it's all a ghastly mistake.

Drink can make us say the silliest of things. My father regularly claims to be the illegitimate son of Field Marshall Montgomery when he's in his cups. Mother always gets embarrassed when he starts, especially in mixed company. Carol's a genuine candidate for Alcoholics Anonymous. I've lost count of the number of times I've seen her pissed out of her brains talking rubbish to some poor victim she's cornered. She's so bloody loud when she starts, so insensitive and snobby and stupid. "If I had my way I'd take the glass out of her hand and slap her face," said the fearless Ian Partington last time we watched her at it. I have to say I agreed with him wholeheartedly at the time. Now here's a mysterious thing. Ronnie always goes into private cubicle when we go into a public toilet for a pee. "I can't piss in the company of strangers," he'll say unfailingly, after. His timidity makes me curious. How big is his dick? Ian Partington, legend in his own lunch-break that he is, claims to have a penis that would make a stallion envious. I'm sceptical. The male member gives more cause for falsehood than any other part of the human anatomy. Is it true, for example, that Napoleon's dickie is preserved in embalming fluid in a bottle somewhere on St. Helena?

Fat uncle Eric, a deceased disreputable brother of my mother, swore blind he'd seen it in a museum while he was doing his national service. Dad still laughs about his claim, always calling Eric "the biggest liar since Adolf Hitler walked the earth" when the story is mentioned. I was fond of Eric. His early death because of hernia complications caused great sadness at the time.

I wonder if Carol's rung her parents to tell them about her suspected complaint, screamed at them over the wires like she screams at us? I've got my doubts. Ronnie says her father's a bishop (or a canon, or something similar). Most clerics I've met try to avoid talking about sexually transmitted diseases. Or maybe it wasn't sexually transmitted at all? Perhaps she got a raw deal at our local blood bank? The health service has certainly declined since my mother got her first hearing aid. I think you're lucky if you can get an aspirin for free these days. Ian Partington, our man about town and expert on almost everything, blames Karl Marx. "If the bearded bastard came down to earth again and saw the problems he's caused he'd jump in the river," is something he always says when discussing the nations health problems. I'm not so sure. Was Karl Marx ever honest enough about himself to remotely consider suicide? Has anybody anywhere read Das Kapital to the end? One day I'll have a try, maybe quote page after page to Partington when he starts to play the expert. I should read more than I do. Ronnie's never without a book, although what he sees in all the horror and science fiction he ploughs through I'll never know. Is Stephen King a person or a computer? I think he must have written more books than any man in the history of the universe. I heard Carol discussing his novels the other day at the bus stop, calling them "rubbish for morons" and "chauvinistic claptrap". The bitterness in her voice shook me to the core. I had no idea she felt so strongly about his work. Sometimes I get the feeling she imagines she's a fount of information on everything. A lot of so-called liberated women of her generation have this problem. My dear old-fashioned Mum calls them "work shy wasters," goes on frequently about "farts who ponce on society." I think she overdoes it a little. It's time she realised we're living in the 1990's and that pretty well anything goes these days. Ian Partington, that wonder of wonders who refuses to entertain the idea that he might be ordinary, met my mother once at a late night party I held for her in my rooms, describing her as "pleasantly truculent with a bird-like manner" - the next day, much to my annoyance. A slight on a member of one's family (no matter how accurate) is something I find hard to tolerate. The urge to kick Partington hard in the balls has been with me for some time now, even if he's supposed to be a friend. Ronnie thinks I'm too excitable, too prone to fly off the handle when pressed, too likely to burst a blood vessel over the tiniest wrong. Maybe he's right? A distant cousin of mine was killed in a pub brawl a couple of years ago. I'll have to watch it. It could be in the genes. And our bad tempered Carol? I've a feeling there's severe madness lurking in her family tree somewhere. Clergymen, according to the supposedly well - informed Ian Partington, are famous for their nutty offspring. I'm not completely sure. All I know is that Martin Luther had a crackpot son who liked exposing himself to nuns and that men of the cloth are said to wear tight underwear when having sexual intercourse. Perhaps the latter has some bearing on the case?

LIFE STORIES

My intelligence will see me through it all. My mince pies are better than his mince pies. What does a turd of man like him know about cooking, fucking, or the noble art of boxing? I'll knock his nose into a creamy fudge.
When (and when oh Lord?) we're all called to the great green pasture in the sky it will be I (and only I) that speaks with him that made us. I've been informed. Chariots of fire have delivered the message to my flirty little dachshunds.

It's five years since I worked properly, five years since I tapped on the typewriter in the basement office of Faggot and Sons. I blame Thomas Archibald Faggot for the current mess I'm in. After all, wasn't it he who put lysergic acid into my morning coffee, set me tumbling, rambling, rollicking on a journey I've never quite recovered from? How cruel our employers can be to us: how negatively overpoweringly powerful. All employment in our little town of Botfield is slavery.
My pathetic reliance on government handouts is the price I pay for rebellion. I can only afford five cartons of milk a week.

My three marriages have all been disasters. Cheryl, the first of my little flock of failures, summed the situation up for herself when she denounced me as, "a baboon born in June who belongs in a crater on the moon." Cheryl was never an advert for sanity. Neither was Karen, the second of the trio, a witch in zip-up furry winter boots and plastic hair curlers. My ears still ring to the sound of her shrill tones. My broken nose is the result of her violence during sex. Josephine was the last of my marital flops. Our divorce, in the depths of winter two years ago, was preceded by a series of vicious snowball fights with her relatives. It was as if they wanted to erase me forever with their balls of soggy, filthy slush. They almost succeeded. The bruises I received took weeks to disappear. Unemployment is a curse that refuses to remove its shadow from me. I'm abused in the street, poked in the ribs by old ladies in the butchers. What is it about my dumpy blob of a figure that makes people so excessive?
A late aunt of mine once said I was born with "trouble in both eyes". She must have been psychic. The left one's been cut and bruised this last week due to a neighbour's child striking me with a giant stick of

rhubarb. This unfounded reputation of mine as a layabout can be traced directly to the vengeful tongues of Josephine and her family. They wish to destroy my every hope, rub my once admired snub of a nose in the shit for all eternity. And why? Can't they accept my third wife's moustache and testicles made normal lovemaking repulsive?

I pride myself on my cooking, baking and the vegetable patch I keep in pristine condition in the back garden. My radishes should have won prizes in the annual Botfield horticultural show. Only the persistent prejudice of the three judges has forced me to fail this past two years. Josephine's kith and kin are everywhere.

My intelligence will confound all who prepare great pits for me to fall into. The excellence of my mince pies will always outshine doughy, lumpy creations. He (and I'm talking about my twin brother who lives in a small shed at the bottom of the garden) has neither the vision nor the vestibule to invalidate me. I will be the first to take tea and jammy sponge cakes with the Saviour when he arrives.

I had a succession of dreams late last year involving King Arthur and three or four of his knights of the round table. When I told my G. P. about them (I was asking him for strong sleeping tablets at the time) he simply shrugged his shoulder, produced an overripe banana from underneath his pullover and sneezed loud enough to wake the dead. "Those that won't work don't get pills," he screeched. "Find yourself suitable employment." As I left his dingy surgery I swept three cactus plants from their emplacements with a wild right arm. "Whoosh," I yelled to the grumpy bunch of waiters (some wearing red bow ties) in the cork-lined waiting room. Their response was complete silence, every particle of it probably motivated by a hatred equal to their loathing of low-tipping dinner guests.

My twin brother took custody of two mangy goats last week. "Could they help with keeping the lawn nice and tidy." I asked on first seeing them, "Save me a job with the lawnmower once in a while?" "No," came the answer, sharp and quick from the deep recesses of his hut. "These goats are holy goats and are here for ceremonial purposes."
"Ceremonial purposes?" I said, adopting a cynical tone. "Yes," he said, and was suddenly silent. Sometimes I think his dodgy set of false teeth

let him down. I'm sure my dead father's pair (for that's who they originally belonged to) don't fit properly. Perhaps he's in permanent pain? He doesn't talk half as much as he should.

Not long ago I toyed briefly with the idea of taking holy orders. When I asked our local vicar here how to go about it he was most discouraging. "The likes of you don't go down well with bishops," he mumbled, one wet evening after evensong. "Your general appearance just doesn't encourage confidence. The average pensioner likes a smartly dressed person to look after his soul."
I was put off. What had my anorak and bell-bottomed jeans got to do with working for Jesus? I felt like punching the pony-tailed, charismatic creep in the face. Only a passing police car prevented me from doing it.
Tomorrow I'm going to look for work. I might go and see Thomas Archibald Faggot, beg him to take me back. I have the kind of brain computers appreciate. Faggot (the maggot!) could use my lust for learning, employ my drug-scarred psyche in a most useful way. I'd give him my body too, if he wanted it. My corpulent form almost begs for researchers to work on it, to cut it up, to dig and delve about. Faggot's surgical appliance company needs new input, a startling visionary to take the lead. I am he.
This life isn't all it should be. I could have been Botfield's very own Rocky Marciano if I'd been given the right advice. Delbert Sugars, my Jamaican trainer from Port Sunlight, put me in the ring with the big boys too early. That six round fight I had with Solly Witherspoon was a disaster for me. I still get strange noises in my right ear. I should have sued him, dragged the fraud through every court in the land.
Danny, the fat plumber from next door, was complimenting me on my radishes at the weekend. "Juicy little swines they are," he said when I met him in the park. I felt so proud I almost broke into tears. Later, after I told that twin brother of mine what Danny had said, he turned all jealous and nasty. "The buggers are too small and they make me shit rotten," he whispered under his breath, his eyes rolling round and a round alarmingly.
I believe my life story would make a very good film. I called somebody in London about it once. It was a disappointing little chat. "Yes," said the woman from the film company before I'd even introduced myself prop-

erly. "Got a little problem with our ego have we? Want to be somebody when we're really nobody at all?" I was practically speechless. All I could say was something trite like, "Thank you for your interest in my project. Shall I leave my name and telephone number?" It was pure humiliation.

I've just had a nasty letter from the council saying my dachshunds might have to be destroyed before summer's out. The postman doesn't like them, sees them as savage little sausages on four legs who should be put to the sword. Can I help it if they like to take a chunk out of a fleshy arse now and then? The public servants in Botfield are tyrants with the power of life and death over God's creatures. Why should a mere postman's complaining result in a death sentence on my three babies? I might write to The Queen and ask for her views on the subject. She's a champion of animal rights isn't she? What if it was one her precious Corgi's was about to be gassed? I'm sure she'd be up in arms about it.

I'm fairly short, a touch paunchy, and have a full head of greying hair. My twin is thin, very small, almost toothless, and wanders around the garden at night teasing the dogs. We are aged fifty-two with eyes of blue. Our mother was a housewife who died young of various cancers. My father, a baker by trade, was run over and killed by a drunken motorist at the age of sixty-eight. We were born and bred in seedy, puritanical, heart of the north, Botfield. All this information about us is probably necessary. The dear reader, for you are he or she, has the right to know as much about what makes us tick as possible. This is my life story and I have to tell the truth. If I lied about Botfield or about the dogs or my brother I'd consider myself a sinner not worth knowing. He that dwells above us sees all. My eldest dachshund sleeps beneath my bed, speaks in tongues; tells me about everything that happens in heaven. I have a direct link to the Saviour through my dogs. They must not be taken away and destroyed.
I'm not insane. A string of doctors have signed documents verifying this fact. Karen, the most foul mouthed of my three ex spouses, spent months trying to convince our G.P. that I was "the maddest, fattest permanently shitfaced bastard in Botfield." She failed - and how! The medical authorities finished up putting her in a secure ward in the local nuthouse after one of her more extreme attacks on my personality. Those that take

pleasure in falsely accusing people should be prepared to be accused themselves.

My intelligence is the cornerstone of my faith in a rosy future. My mince pies (especially at Christmas time) will always rise above the opposition; forever beat my brother's soggy efforts into a cocked hat. And if he wants to start a ruckus in the garden, I'm ready. My daily walk around the duck pond with the dachshunds has kept me fitter than he'll ever be.

2

They call me Lionel. He didn't mention my name. I'm the one that lives in the wooden hut at the bottom of our long, long garden. I believe that he, the one who calls himself my brother and twin, is two or three bricks short of a full load. He talks of baking mince pies, though he's never baked so much as a jam tartlet in his life. He goes on about being an excellent gardener but the garden here's a jungle, a tangle of scraggy briars, nettle clumps and assorted old tyres. And the goats I'm accused of purchasing? It's a lie. What would I want with treacherous creatures like those? I'd rather keep vampire bats in my bedroom - if I had one.

My so-called brother is generally known as Terry, Terry the nut from the pit of hell. The silly billy has been in and out of mental institutions for years. He has fantasies, long periods when he becomes someone other than himself. Around Christmas he thought he was Sir Stanley Matthews, the renowned footballer of yesteryear. He was out in the deep snow practicing with his ball for days. I couldn't get a sensible word out of him. He refused to eat anything but boiled eggs and fresh orange slices right until Christmas Eve. And the farting! I don't think I've ever come across a human being with so much wind in them. Even Lottie, my former wife who left me for a communist, couldn't have matched him. The stink and the volume were incredible. Neighbours remarked on it. A man from the public health office was called on three separate occasions.

Dachshunds can be difficult if their owner kisses and coddles them too much. Pinky, Potter and Rasputin should be put down. Terry's "little sweetie pies" (as he insists on calling them) are the terrors of the neighbourhood. I can't lay my underpants out to dry on the wild rosebush by my hut for fear of one them chewing them up. What's the world coming to when a grown man can't control three or four legged Frankfurters with bad tempers? I can't wait till the authorities finally put their foot down. The idyllic life I planned for myself isn't working out at all.
We used to be the best of friends, Terry and me. Ten years ago we were inseparable, seen together in every pub, club and betting shop in the Botfield area. Then he started taking drugs. L.S.D. became his cruel taskmaster, his eventual, hateful, horrible downfall. He went from good trips to bad trips, spent every last penny of his hard earned cash on the

rubbish. It was while tripping he decided I was his twin. It was while tripping he ordered me out of the cosy little house we'd shared for two years and forced me to live in the shed at the bottom of the garden. I'm not an aggressive man. I didn't try to resist. My idea was that he was sick, would eventually come to his senses; perhaps allow me back into the house again when he felt better. What a foolish, over optimistic dreamer I was. Terry's madness has gradually worsened over the last decade (despite his abstinence from drugs for some years now). The lying, cheating, objectionable beast within him has gradually taken over his soul. I'm afraid of him. I rarely leave my hut during daylight hours.

My hut is my refuge. The world could explode, implode, or simply vanish in a great firestorm, and that little home of mine would somehow survive. I want to die in it, breath my very last breath while smiling up through its one tiny window at the rooks and starlings that gather to greet me there. All feathered creatures are my associates, friends and protectors. Without their timely warnings Terry's fat little dogs would have had me for breakfast long ago.

I'm a neat and tidy sort. My possessions are my pride. The collection of clocks, ladies watches and egg-timers I've acquired over the years frequently draw astonished gasps of admiration from visitors. Callers have been few of late. Terry gets abusive when he spots someone knocking on my door, shouts out things like, "Watch the little arsehole doesn't poison you," and "kick him up his fat bottom if he bends over." People are put off. It's bloody difficult to make appointments these days. Word has got round. Size bothers me a lot. I pray every night for a magical occurrence that will turn me into a man of respectable height. If I was bigger I could reduce Terry to a whimpering fool, force him to recognise my rights as an equal partner. I don't want to be the butt of his cruel humour. I need to know he's going to keep Pinky, Potter and Rasputin under firm control. Life's a can full of writhing, blood-sucking worms. To be vertically challenged can result in a simple trip to the supermarket turning into a treacherous journey through the minefield of human aggression. Only last week an overweight female of about six years pelted me with eggs and tomatoes taken from her mother's shopping trolley. The humiliation involved in such an incident can leave horrendous scars, both emotionally and physically. It took nearly a whole bottle of the best shampoo to get all the sticky egg yolk out of my hair afterwards.

Does God visit the unemployed, has he the will and compassion to give succour to a small, frequently unhappy person deep into the middle of his life? If he decided to come I'd bake him top quality mince pies, soak his tired feet in a bowl of soothing warm water drawn from the trusty old boiler that stands by my bed. All I have would be his (even my little bedside lamp that sometimes fails because of my poor electricity supply). The King of the universe would be welcomed like a King, treated with the respect his holy personage, we are told, demands.

And if there were angels, spiritual concubines etc. accompanying him? Simple. They would have to sleep in the garden, brave the beastly dachshunds; close their ears to Terry's endless ranting.

3

Now it's my turn! I'm a chap just returned from six long months in Botfield's very own mental institution. Most of my friends call me Dickie. I'm strong, handsome, perfectly formed around the biceps and stomach. Both Lionel and Terry are former friends of mine. I want to speak (even if you don't want me to) about their odd behaviour these past few years, try to get to the core of what makes them tick.
It has to be remembered, first of all, that neither of them were born normal, that both were irascible arseholes almost from day one. Their mother (Yes, they are twins) was a rapscallion from the gloomy innards of dirty old Botfield. It was rumoured, by many, that she collected old bottles for their deposit, made a pitiful living at it. I suspect this story to be a rotten falsehood. How does one find the cash to build a four bedroomed house in the suburbs of Botfield? Not by collecting dusty beer and lemonade bottles on a handcart, I'm sure. No, the answer's simple: prostitution. Old Nellie Latchworth, in her day, was the most delightful piece of female flesh in the whole of Botfield. My father, a former mayor of this town, was a secret customer of hers for years. He told me all about it on his deathbed. His Catholic upbringing demanded that he confessed all to all and sundry before he passed on. The tales of debauchery that issued from his cracked and festering lips defy the telling.

Lionel and Terry have been neighbours of mine for almost six years. Up to three years ago I used to be Lionel's regular drinking partner. It was always me who used to order his booze for him (he couldn't see over the bar to attract the barman's attention). I was readily available to assist whenever assisting was necessary. Oh Lionel loved his gin and tonic, would regularly stagger back to that silly hut of his blind drunk. How he managed to buy so much alcohol on social security payouts is a mystery to me. Perhaps his mother (she died of various cancers) left him something in her will? I should have asked him but I didn't want to pry. I'm not the nosy sort.

Until a year ago, a Wednesday night piss-up with Terry was a regular occurrence. I don't think there was an alcoholic beverage he didn't consume. He was a little bloated fish with a raging thirst. I was his captive audience, as he rambled on about his differences with his twin. I was an alcoholic and he was an alcoholic. Those expensive days and nights spent in pubs, nightclubs and any old smelly cellar that would sell drink eventually led to my downfall. When I'm hung-over, searching through the dustbin in the kitchen for a beer can with a few drops in it, I curse blokes like Terry and Lionel. I was only a casual weekend imbiber until I met them. Bad influences can sour the sweetest of human beings. I've become a tyrannical wolf of man with a taste for wearing female underwear on a regular basis because of people like the twins. I'm topped up to the brim with hate. I explode into a flurry of arms, legs and dangling, swinging private parts (I exaggerate!) without any warning at all. Only pills keep me from going under completely.

Botfield has one of the finest mental institutions. Dr. Edward Ramsbottom, head psychiatrist and former England rugby international, leads one of the most efficient medical teams known to mankind. His books, fourteen of which I've read in the past six months, cover subjects as varied as brain surgery and first-aid for sick and psychotic pets. Our small town is lucky to have such a man as a citizen. The medication he provides has kept potential psychotics like me out of trouble for weeks at a time. Now, for instance, I can visit the supermarket without causing an unpleasant scene. Now, given the right weather conditions, I can play football with the local kids without stealing the ball.
I wished I could find a job. Work is something I desperately need. In these parts, when a man reaches middle age he's only good for the scrap heap. I've applied for situation after situation without so much as a sniff. Last week I went for an interview for a job as a lifesaver at the public swimming baths, only told my muscles were too prominent (I took my shirt off to show the boss there the wondrous state of my biceps: a mistake) and that my grey hair spoilt the groovy young image they were trying to promote of themselves. No wonder my drinking's increased these past few years. Thank God I can still work out in the living room when I'm sober. Thank God my trusty barbells and chest-expanders haven't been pawned yet.
What is pure madness? Have I been half mad, possibly? There's a groaning in my sacred soul that tells me I'll have to leave Botfield shortly. The Terry's and Lionel's of this mixed-up universe are a real danger. My sanity depends on me setting up home as far away from them as possible. "But Dickie," a friend of mine said to me some days ago, after I'd told

him my plan. "Why do you have to leave? The twins haven't crossed your path for years." Then I rambled on about my fears of permanent insanity, alcoholism, dreams I have of Terry and Lionel stuffing sticks of rhubarb into my mouth while I'm sleeping. My friend snorted with laughter, thumped the kitchen table with his hairy fists. "You silly bugger," he almost screamed, "those twins only live four doors down the road. Couldn't you just pop round and settle your differences? What did they do to you to make you so paranoid?"
It was useless. How could an insurance salesman (for that's what my friend is) be expected to unravel or even vaguely appreciate the complexities of an unemployed body builder? In fact, how could anybody on this earth (and that includes Dr. Ramsbottom) fully understand the humiliation I suffered at the hands of those twins; I did my best and they all but defecated over me. To be called a sponger, a bore and a closet homosexual by such types causes pain. I now know I'll have to take tablets for the rest of my life.

4

As a family doctor, one naturally comes across many bizarre and interesting cases. Lionel and Terry, for instance, are prize examples of the stranger than strange. I've almost lost count the number of times I've had to call the police to eject Terry from my premises. "Botfield's not big enough for the two of us Doc," were the last words he spoke to me before he went off to Cleethorpes for his holiday last year. I haven't seen or heard of him since. Perhaps he's intimidated by the former wrestler and Royal Marine I've employed to guard me these past three months? A man in my position has to feel secure at all times. Lionel still rings now and then though, waffles on boringly about Jesus Christ, Sir Stanley Matthews, the hanging breasts of my young secretary. I tolerate it as much as I can, but won't allow him into my surgery. The last time he paid us a visit he nearly strangled my wife when she tried to give him an injection.

Dickie Dorset is another problem patient of mine. His overweight mother, who died of a heart attack in the town's main shopping centre some years ago, gave him everything he wanted when he was a child: chocolates, endless packets of bubble gum, water pistols, plastic howitzers... everything.

No wonder he's developed self-motivation difficulties. The need to get up off his backside and forage for himself very rarely occurs to him. The wibbly, wobbly shadow of his mother follows him around to this day.

I don't think I'm being unfair if I say Botfield's got more than its share of human oddities. For instance, Dr. Ramsbottom, local psychiatrist and would-be guru, isn't all he's cracked up to be. Has anybody anywhere, for example, heard of the University of Lower Manitoba, the highly respected (according to Dr. Ramsbottom) centre of academic excellence, where the good doctor is supposed to have studied for his numerous degrees? I haven't, and neither has my wife Maria. She says, and I believe she's right, that he fooled the hospital board at Botfield with a combination of "good looks, pseudo scientific horseshit, and a fake Yankee accent." It's a scandal? I've tried exposing the charlatan on frequent occasions, protested loudly at town council meeting, written several (unpublished) articles for the Botfield Gazette, but to no avail. Botfield adores its Dr. Ramsbottom, apparently can't heal its stinking and sordid body and soul without him.

For those who like the details of a person's background to be revealed in detail, who enjoy penetrating the mists of privacy, I'm certainly not your man. Talking about my past life would involve exposing too many secrets of national and international importance to close scrutiny. I think it's enough to state that I was once in espionage. As Maria, my lapsed Catholic Italian wife of the past five years, often says, "First they take your soul and then they take your house." I'm sixty-one years old and met my spouse in Pisa on a camping holiday. It's my third stab at marriage.

Last night (or was it the night before?) some Jehovah's witnesses were causing a nuisance at my surgery door yelling, "We have a place in heaven for you," in chorus through the intercom. It was late and I was deadly tired. Maria was massaging my legs as I lay on the couch. "Is Orpheus really part of the underworld," she inquired as she stroked and rubbed and stroked. "Do the primroses in their little plastic pots have interesting conversations with the cucumbers in their frames?" I let out a weary gasp then broke wind ferociously, sadly causing Maria to flinch at the volume. "Could you turn that bloody intercom off?" I asked, with a menace in my voice that surprised me, "Those religious maniacs are driving me nuts."

Maria obeyed, her beautiful powdered nose twitching at the stink of my fart, her face a study in puzzlement as she returned to the couch. "Maria Callas had difficulties with her lower bowel," she whispered, crossing her legs with unusual rapidity. "Things started to go wrong after she'd passed forty. I think she noticed stains on the sheets after a performance of Tosca in Milan. They say a doctor was called, examined her, and told her the worst in the back garden of her villa three days later."

"There's nothing wrong with your lower parts," I said, smiling encouragingly, a little confused by the subject under discussion. "I know," she replied, taking a hatpin out of a pocket in her blouse and jabbing hard into my left thigh, the wickedest of smiles on her thirty-five years old, spoilt brat of a face.

Botfield is a swim with bibulous types. Father Micklewight-Moody, for example, spends far more time in The Goat and Trumpet, than is good for his health. The tale is rife around town of him collapsing in a slobbering heap while in the midst of communion one Sunday. I'm sure there's more than a grain of truth in it. I've seen him dead to the world on a least three occasions in the supermarket car park – penis half out of his trousers, his weekend shopping strewn around for anybody to steal. Is it any wonder Maria's lost all interest in church matters? The Lord deserves more reliable people to go about his daily business for him. As my mother-in-law frequently said before she embarked on that last great journey. "If Jesus isn't boss in his own church, then you might as well turn it over to the pigeons." Wisdom or wit were qualities I never associated with the impolite ratbag. Her bursts of potty erudition always surprised me.

5

I believe that Mullarkey should be horsewhipped for telling so many dreadful lies about me. The job of a man of God can be irksome at the best of times without the Mullarkeys of this world falsifying the moral accounts. That G.P. was on the phone a couple of hours ago trying to persuade me to drop by his surgery. When I inquired as to why, he babbled on about me making a fool of myself in the supermarket forecourt. Where does the interfering bourgeois busybody get his info from? I lay the blame firmly at the feet of Arthur Thomas Mullarkey, my former gardener. That nosy son of an incorrigible Irish pickpocket has never had a good word to say for me since I nearly got him excommunicated for stealing tulip bulbs. Yes, this ongoing conflict, this cloud of nastiness that hovers me, started with some sinful thieving that I felt duty bound to report to Bishop O'Hara. Why has God treated me so shabbily for my diligence?

I'm a Micklewight-Moody from a long line of highly religious Micklewight-Moody's. My cousin Ernest, the only Micklewight-Moody to cross the Atlantic to Oklahoma and take holy orders, once had himself symbolically crucified outside Botfield railway station in protest at the raising cost of dairy butter and those little rubbery cheese triangles. "I did it for the pensioners," he said to the sympathetic policeman afterwards. A Micklewight-Moody will never tolerate bare-faced injustice. Cheese triangles and dairy butter have a special place in old people lives. Who are these filthy rich dairymen who want to deprive them of their pleasures? Boiling in oil is too good for them. And there's more.
Another cousin of mine, a nursing nun living rough somewhere in the wilds of Togo, is reportedly directly in line for sainthood. It's wonderful. Interesting reports have been filtering back to my diocese for years now about her hut building programmes, latrine digging and huge appetite for self-flagellation. The Micklewight-Moody is nothing if not determined. A steeplejack second cousin of mine once wrestled a polar bear in the nude for church charities.

Teddy and Lionel Latchworth sometimes attend evening Benediction. Neither are Catholics, but who gives a twopenny toss these days?

Changing the subject…
The last time I had a lengthy chat with Bishop O'Hara he said he was seriously considering opening a free seafood stall in our cathedral close. "It'll draw all those sweet stray lambs into the fold," he whispered, a slight quiver of doubt revealing itself in his high-pitched voice.

The Latchworth twins never attend church together. A long standing argument (Dr Ramsbottom told me all about it once but I've forgotten the cause) keeps them permanently at odds with each other. Terry's more religious than Lionel though, given to muttering about "personal contact with the Saviour" at the drop of a hat. I don't discourage him. Everyone's entitled to find their own way to Paradise. Balls to the Pontiff and his narrow-minded coven in Rome. Only bigoted die-hards pay any attention to their doomy way of going on.
I'm a strange one though, aren't I? One minute I'm holding forth about freedom and liberalism in the church and the next moment I'm reporting Mullarkey to the bishop for stealing a few tulip bulbs. I guess you could say I'm an enigma. My red velvet waistcoat is forever drawing adverse comments at parish council meetings.

I was talking to one of my senior altar servers last Sunday about Mullarkey's plotting, about his poisoning my name all over the parish. His compassionate response to the plight I'm in lifted my spirits sky high. It isn't very often a humble parish priest is called "a saint without equal in the battle for human souls."
I went about my business with a new found fervour for the rest of that day. The insight of an eighteen year old in the service of Jesus can often be touchingly supportive.

Dr Ramsbottom came to see me about that unemployed, lapsed Catholic neighbour of mine Dickie Dorset last week, inquiring if Mullarkey's old gardening job was available. I had to turn the idea down. Dickie was a never ending cause of trouble and strife at the parish youth club in his younger days, once almost strangling a novice nun after losing to her in a table-tennis match. The sight of his tanned, muscular upper body at a recent charity swimming gala brought back terrible memories, sent the proverbial shivers up my spine.

I should forgive but I can't .The Lord made me a coward and that's how he prefers me to stay. I think Dr. Ramsbottom understood, what a gentleman! I always think a university education brings out the best in a man.

Sometimes I imagine how it would have been if I'd married and had a family. Would I have been happier than I am now? There was a little poppet I fancied before I took myself off to the seminary: cherubic, cheeky and just a touch overweight, she was my version of a dream girl. Sadly, The Lord doesn't always provide us with what we lust after. The relationship broke down at a bowling alley in Botfield after I admitted to having bleeding haemorrhoids. Her intolerance (she called me a nineteen year old with the arse of a pensioner) rocked me to the core. My faith in God was torn into shreds for weeks and weeks afterwards. Only my mother's nightly pep talks saw me through.

My G.P. is a sworn enemy of all things Catholic. The last time I paid a visit to his surgery (haemorrhoids again) he felt it his duty to lecture me on "the evils of papist thinking," while all the time prodding at my exposed anus with cotton buds. I wouldn't have minded so much if his wife, an ex-parishioner of mine - the former Maria Bagotti, hadn't been in attendance. Her sniggering at my discomfort was a monstrous emotional imposition on a servant of The Lord. It took prolonged meditation in front of the crucifix (at least three hours of it before I got into bed that night) to remove the stain of hatred from my soul. Maria is now an enemy that I love. Tolerance is the greatest virtue of all.

A favourite niece of mine, is always wanting to know what heaven is like. What can a gum chewing ten year old with a puzzled look on her chubby face want when she asks this kind of question? That paradise is a vast public park full of dull but smiling people in white robes, that our heavenly reward is to live in a tedious land of nowhere without T.V., C.D's or fat juicy hamburgers? My job's incredibly tough at times. How can I talk with knowledge and insight about a place I've never visited? Young people expect far too much these days.

Another question that's frequently asked by the more conservative members of my congregation concerns my good friend Dr. Ramsbottom. Oh dear, oh dear. Why does this bunch of so-called Christians make accusations that have no basis in truth? Why does the question "Is he gay?" trip so easily from so many tongues when the illustrious doctor is around? When asked I usually shake my head furiously in very positive denial, often contriving to form my lips into a "How disgusting" kind of sneer in order to add extra weight to my position on the matter. However, I want it to be known I'm not against homosexuality. Two distant cousins of mine in far away Australia regularly work as male strippers in the Sidney gay bars. This Micklewight-Moody clan I proudly belong to is liberal-minded, God fearing and morally eccentric. Our intentions are always honourable.

6

The job of a psychiatrist, in my much sought after opinion, is to light up those shadows in the mind that refuse to be lit up, to offer pills, succour and a metaphysical kick up the arse to the spiritually scarred. My numerous qualifications hang prominently in all four rooms of my well appointed workplace. Life's so good to me. I'm proud to be well loved by my dear patients and pleased as Punch to be thought of so highly in some medical circles. Is there anyone out there with a more fulfilling occupation? One of my favourite patients, the unemployed bodybuilder and depressive Mr. Dickie Dorset, perhaps said it all when he called me "God's own wondrous worker of earthly miracles" over the phone last week. I thank God every night that Valium works for him. His delusions (particularly about the frequently obnoxious Latchworth twins) cause him more sadness than we normal people could ever begin to envisage. No wonder he hasn't been able to get a proper job of late. I'm Dr. Edward Ramsbottom (if you hadn't already guessed) lover of life, ludicrously expensive holidays and attractive young women. I've never married but I'm available for offers. Yes, the years have gone by but I haven't, as yet, come across a ripe and tasty morsel that I could turn into a wife. I'm hopeful though. It took years for Mick Jagger to settle down properly. My mid fifties are a delight. I laughed my head off at dinner the other evening when my beefy young colleague Jack Crowberry said, "Fun's your middle name Eddie. When do you find time to sleep?" I've often wondered how I keep it up myself. Play hard and work harder – that's my motto! How else should a chap in my responsible position live?

Every pillar of society has his enemies. My principal opponent in this town of Botfield is that drear jealous old turd of a G. P. Ralph Hancock. Has there ever been a bigger bag of wind let loose on a civilized community? Every fibre of my being twitches and itches when his name is mentioned. His ceaseless attacks on my reputation have now gone far beyond a joke. Even the Rev. Micklewight-Moody, a tolerant and saintly fellow most of the time, has had enough of Hancock's constant name calling, referring to the cursed G.P. as "our devilish adversary" last time we took tea together. And Hancock's bug infested drone of a wife? The image of her queening around the town's shopping centre – all flounce, bounce and mutton dressed as lamb – is a nightmare that occurs on a weekly basis. Why does she always have to do her shopping when I'm doing my shopping? Who encourages her to scream "spastic homo" into my face each time I stand next to her in the checkout queue? Something has to be done. Maybe my good friend Dickie Dorset will snap her neck in two for me next time he's in town? All I have to do is change his drug prescription. Turning a depressive into a psychopath isn't that difficult. Come to think of it, I could get him to snuff out the evil Hancock while he's at it. He always leaves his living room windows open in summer. Any nutcase could climb in.

I'm due to take a long, well deserved, holiday in about two weeks. The hoi polloi and their mental traumas are going to have to take a back seat to fun, giggles and my snorkelling goggles for a while. I adore exploring the shoals of exotic fish and uniquely interesting plant life under the deep, mysterious oceans of the world. If I hadn't qualified as a noted psychiatrist I'd have probably taken up deep sea diving for a living. I'm told there's a ton of money in hunting for lost treasure, that to spend ones life in tight rubber suiting can be excessively rewarding. Anyway, it's the gleaming white beaches of Barbados for me this year. I might ask my young chum Jack Crowberry along for the trip. We could search for pretty girls together.

I was looking hard into my full-length bedroom mirror yesterday. The sight that greeted me pleased me to the marrow of every bone in my well-sculpted form! I'm handsome! I heard myself shouting to the little Polaroid of my mother that's pinned over my bed! I have the powerful dignity of a Greek god! It was the most magic of magic moments I could have sworn mother's purple velvet hat (with those oh so ghastly cherries) moved slightly to the right, as if acknowledging my special state of being. Is it any wonder that some of the female inmates of our well-appointed hospital feel moved to throw themselves at my feet when I pass? It's one hell of a feeling to know I'm me.

7

Now, attentive reader, you need an overview, a voice that can steady the ship. I'm the man. They call me Derek Grimby, chief inspector Grimby from Botfield's ruthlessly efficient central police station. My job is my life. My underwear, for I'm deprived of a skilful wife since my Kathleen popped off, is consistently in a parlous state. The seamstress in me won't come out. My efforts to patch and renew things always end in a botch of a job

Have you ever wished yourself to be something other than what you are, schemed like a psycho through sleepless nights to change the patterns in your life? I haven't. My resolve, apart from sometimes shilly-shallying over the correct colour of pullover to wear on a mild winter's morning, has never been anything less than firm. I always wanted to be a police officer, always yearned for the hat, the nightstick, the pistol concealed beneath the flak jacket. My mother said it best when I was eight years old. "He's got the build of a perfect Sherlock Holmes", she snapped proudly to a friend one afternoon at a handicapped person's gala, all he needs is one of those funny pipes to smoke. The dear woman was a natural psychic, predicting her own death by drowning at Cleethorpes two and a half years later being her crowning achievement.

I'm a top-class judge of character Lionel and Terry Latchworth, for example, are a perfect pair of sibling rivals. Their pettiness astounds me. I've lost count of the times I've been called out to that curious household of theirs. One day they'll hack each other to death.

Dickie Dorset's a layabout. His mother spoilt him, took away all independence, turned him into a crawling, muscular cry-baby with the heart and soul of a stuffed rabbit. He's a fiasco. He could have been a leading male model if he'd applied himself to it.

And Ralph Hancock, everybody's least favourite, but apparently necessary G.P.? He's straight and without blemish as far as I'm concerned. A bigot, a bullshitter and a gossip of the most loathsome kind, but unreachable. He hasn't even got a traffic offence against his name. And Maria, his ever-loving but unlovable loudmouth, of a foreign wife? The same. Peachy clean.

Not a single blob on her dago passport, not the slightest whisper of alleged criminal inclinations from any quarter. It's a source of rage and almost scandal at headquarters. We'd love to haul them in for questioning but can't. Driven snow couldn't be whiter than that smarty pair.

Micklewight-Moody should be put away. Him and his family are a danger to public health, morals and possibly nervous young mothers with impressionable youngsters. How the hell did a nut like him gain the qualifications to become a priest? There must be some weird and wonderful codgers in the Vatican. Thank God I'm not of the Catholic faith. I suspect they lace the communion wine with cheap brandy. Micklewight-Moody stank to high heaven last time I met him in the bookmakers. I've heard he frequently drives that old Fiat of his when he's over the odds. I'd love to catch him out. His arse would be on fire after I'd finished kicking it. Botfield needs clean living priests with pure, chaste minds. Micklewight-Moody is a wrong-headed let down. I pity those rubicund-cheeked altar servers of his. One day I'll arrest the swine, lock him up and throw away the key I'll make sure he doesn't get close to innocent youth again.

And then there's the much maligned Dr. Ramsbottom. Is he a fake? Is he tinkering with the minds of Botfield's populace without the suitable diplomas? I've heard he's into black magic, isn't averse to casting spells on people who piss him off. I'll have to be careful if I decide to dig into his past. P.C. Warnock, one of our most capable officers, told me he once investigated a suspected phoney fortune-teller who put the evil eye on him afterwards. "Couldn't achieve an erection for six months," he whined after I asked him for details, "my wife almost started divorce proceedings." If anyone doubts a policeman's lot can sometimes be very trying then Warnock's fate should be an eye-opener. I detest those folk who think we spend most of our time lurking around the station drinking cocoa and sending out for pizzas. We give good value for the tax payers money. I was bitten twice in the left buttock by an excitable young bullmastiff when I first started in this job.

I'm often asked if I'm seeking a replacement for my sweet dead wife, Kathleen.
It's a problem. In the past few weeks I've discovered I'm a transvestite

and can't stop lusting after pretty frocks and high-heeled bootees. I'm partially ashamed, partially elated. My greatest fear is becoming a pariah, a strain and liability to my fellow officers. Derek Grimby will never become Doris Grimby. My secret must remain firmly embedded within, forever.

8

I am what I am.
My conquest of the inner mind will see me through it all. Botfield and its mangy inhabitants will never ever grind me down. Lionel, that half-arsed shit of a brother of mine, will have to be made to disappear. I have the means to do it. The glorious god of glorious unreason has spoken to me. Mother Teresa has been communicating. And can we live as friends on this piss heap of a planet of ours?
All the saints in heaven (and that includes the dapper snappy Teresa) say NO.
My mince pies are crunchy yet smooth inside, a fair treat for the eyes and stomach. If I confuse you it's because the room is silent and everyone's talking at once. The shadows quiver to the sound of high octave arguing. This story you read is my story. I made it up. How are you to know if my twin exists? How can you find out if I'm really Terry Latchworth? And Dickie Dorset and Dr.Ramsbottom and Micklewight-Moody and Ralph Hancock (and wife) and the kinky Grimby.... are they real?
I wade through dog turds in a garden that has become hell's landscape.
I see a primitive shed with a single light bulb twitching through a curtain less window. Have I to break the door down and murder the occupant?

Last night I heard Rocky Marciano talking to Delbert Sugars about Dr.Hancock. Three nights ago I thought I heard that sneaky swine Grimby telling lies about Dickie Dorset to a woman with a laugh in her voice. Danny the plumber emerged from the broom cupboard yesterday. "Everything's fine and dandy", he said as he brushed past me.
"I love the air of gentle relaxation that fills this abode." Ah, it never stops in this place. Night after night I play dominoes with myself in the kitchen in an attempt to prevent myself thinking about daggers, guns, Molotov cocktails. A rare type of indoor creeping plant has started to take hold in my bathroom. Soon I'll be showering amidst green leaves, little yellow flowers with pink centres. Paradise, it seems, is about to reveal itself in the place where I wash and shit. There are hints of a better kind of existence almost everywhere. "A solution", shouts a bitter and twisted voice in my right ear, "there has to be an end to all of this."

"There isn't," I answer aloud, weakly. "There can never be."
The truth is I have a sequence of wires (starting at the tip top of my right ear) that run through my body and legs and make direct contact with mother earth.
When I stamp my feet the street lights of Botfield can be suddenly extinguished. I've spoken to Dr.Ramsbottom about it and he's taken notes.

RABBIT TEETH

He that has rabbit teeth must surely perish in the fires of ignominy. To be less than perfectly attractive in this shitpit of a world is (and always will be) a cardinal sin.
My bones are unusual and precious though. I am to be a victim of grave robbers when I die.
Oh sorry.
I'm a bit out of sorts lately. I get stupid when stressed.

This week finds me on holiday in Bournemouth with a Welsh cousin from Egypt. It's "Boyo" this and "Boyo" that throughout the day and, to tell the truth, I'm sick to the back of my outrageous teeth with it. I don't want to wallow in his Welshness.
He's an Egyptian as far as I'm concerned. The dark blue fez he wears in bed gives him away.

I'm joking about my bones.
What would any self-respecting grave robber want with a working-man like me? My Egyptian cousin says that rabbit teeth signify great wisdom and possible prophetic skills.
I keep telling him he's talking out of his buttocks but he just laughs. His laughter is loud enough to unhinge all the fish in the Nile, start pyramids collapsing, cause yashmaks to flutter in a stiff breeze. It's a bugger of a thing, an impudent tornado that has to be stopped. Our holiday is being spoilt because of it.
Yesterday, at breakfast, he made my boiled egg explode, sent both my pieces of thickly buttered toast flying through the dining room window. It was a small incident, but somehow sad. I couldn't eat a thing afterwards. My appetite was lost in a fog of insecurity.

There are three of us on this holiday: me, Cedric (my would be Welsh cousin) and Ali, a half brother of mine from Kilmarnock, Scotland.
We're taking this break together because we were all born on the same day in 1952. Strange, isn't it?
Ali, who has one leg and breeds canaries for a living, calls us the "Dynamic Trio," I tend to disagree.

There's a feeble quality about us that scares me slightly. I have a gut feeling we'll all die of cancer in trying circumstances.

The weather's been shocking this week. I've been soaked to the skin so many times Ali's taken to calling me, "Mr Mackintosh of the squelching shoes." I find him just a touch insensitive. Would he like it if he got drenched to his underpants every time he strolled down the promenade? I asked him yesterday if he'd consider lending me his umbrella occasionally. His answer surprised, hurt and baffled me.
"Buy your own bloody umbrella," he almost shouted. "I know you've got more money in your post office account than King Farouk. Spend it!"
Cedric, who was standing with us in the T.V. room at the time, almost split his big fat belly with laughter. I suppose it was the reference to King Farouk. Anything Egyptian tickles him pink.

I've had a lot of spare time to think seriously about life this summer. Both Cedric and Ali are lighthearted types. I sometimes wish I could be like them. My musing amuses them. My yellow rain hat – big, plastic and utterly practical – has them falling to the floor and laughing like demented epileptics. Could it be I'm a sort of clown to them? Last night I sobbed with despair under the sheets for almost one and a half hours. Neither Cedric nor Ali heard me. They were eating fish and chips by the pier at the time. This is the third time we've been on holiday together. I don't think I'll join in next year.
Sharing a room with two permanently amused alcoholics can be horrible. Cedric's laughter, always a constant threat, caused my new tube of toothpaste to splurt out all its contents over my dressing gown this morning. Ali, who was sitting on the toilet playing furiously with himself at the time, laughed so much he was sick on my socks.
What is it about myself that makes me such an attractive target for life's little accidents?
Is it my insistence on sleeping with a spare pair of underpants and a clean handkerchief under my pillow? Cedric's always calling me "a miserable bastard" for not joining in with the fun and games.
How would he like it if somebody puked on his best pair of tartan socks? I'm beginning to hate this holiday. I left half a sausage and a whole tomato on my plate at breakfast. Thank God we've got single beds.

I had my portrait painted last year. The artist, a close friend of mine from schooldays, did a marvellous job, reducing my rabbit teeth to normal size and putting a thatch of hair on my balding pate that would have done credit to the most flamboyant of teddy boys. My mother, bless her wizened eighty-two year old heart, didn't think much of it though.
"Makes you look like a pimp," was all she could mutter when I showed her the work. Sometimes I wish I'd married. Living at home can be a curse at my age.

Cedric and Ali have announced they're going shopping for holiday mementoes in the town centre tomorrow afternoon. I think I'll give it a miss. Ali has a proclivity for pinching female bottoms; all sizes, all shapes. I don't want to get arrested. My freedom means more to me than anything; a succulent battered fish and a carton of mushy peas don't enter into it.

Being free also means I can watch Derby County on Saturday afternoons. Could any activity on God's turbulent earth be worth missing my favourite football team in action for? Cedric and Ali are like two giggling juveniles.
I've got a responsible job canning peaches, baby asparagus and marrowfat peas. My position as foreman in control of foreign exports must not be threatened in any way.

Cedric's obsessed with Cardiff.
"The city of the gods," he calls it, "a paradise for men, children and all women over fifty." I've a powerful suspicion he's never been near the place. My mother says he was born in Cairo, and I have to admit, he certainly looks like someone from the dark continent when he's got his fez on. It's very strange, very peculiar, very disturbing to a suave and honest chap like myself. I wish he'd stop calling me "Boyo," in front of the guests in the dining room. Listening to Ali's tales of loose women, pregnant canaries and a one legged nun from Sri Lanka is more than enough for one sensitive man to bear.

Does perfect peace exist? Can underpants and vests be worn in such a way that facile comment becomes a thing of the past? The sea is wild today. Both Cedric and Ali have gone sailing. Our boarding house land-

lady forecast "many deaths in the cruel waters" in the T.V. room earlier today. I shouldn't be negative, but I am. What if Margaret Schultz, part-time psychic and keeper of the cleanest dog kennels masquerading as hotels on this stretch of coastline, turns out to be stunningly right? I have a sudden, sharply focused picture in my head of two bloated corpses floating towards distant continents, ravenous seagulls pecking at their private parts. My mother has always said I lack compassion. Maybe if she'd been threatened by mocking laughter for most of her adult life she'd hold another point of view?
I wish the worst for my tormentors.

It's well past two o'clock in the early hours and my fellow holidaymakers haven't returned. It's eerie here. This little room, the scene of more than a dozen farting contests in the past two weeks, is unusually cold for the time of the year. Downright strangeness rules the night. The television, a source of endless irritation during my stay here, refuses to be switched off or unplugged; plays a mournful sea shanty through its grey, blank screen. I think I see a seagull waddling round the bathroom. Unseen forces pull at the tassel on my pyjamas. Am I to lose my virginity to the shadows? Then I hear my two companions staggering drunkenly up the stairs.
"Little fat mummy's boy seems to be asleep," shouts Cedric to his legless chum as they half crawl through the door. "Thank God we're going home soon. Have you smelt his socks? They stink like shit gone bad."
My doomy mood ceases almost immediately. Reality's wet flannel strikes me hard in the middle of the face and, for some strange reason, I'm faintly relieved.

We're leaving for home at midday tomorrow. A strange golden light is casting grotesque shapes on our room's lurid pink wallpaper as I pack. I imagine the spirit world is trying to reach me in some way. Could the devil and Jesus Christ be fighting a battle for my soul in Bournemouth this very second? Cedric hung himself in the bathroom last night. I was the one who removed his fez when they cut him down. Should I pack it with the rest of my stuff, take it back with me as a keepsake? They're going to miss him on the vegetable stall he part owned in Cairo. His partner screamed like a wild animal when I rang and informed him of the tragedy ten minutes ago.

Ali told me at breakfast that Cedric was addicted to aspirins and always wore his underpants back to front because of an obscure Muslim custom he'd learnt at school.

"What nonsense," was all I could say to the whispered information. Cedric's untimely death had obviously scrambled Ali's brain. The egg yolk down the front of his pullover spoke volumes. His unsteady hand suggested a partial stroke. The redoubtable Mrs Schultz recognised his condition immediately, took him – limping badly, slobbering at the mouth – into the street for fresh air.

I heard the seagulls greet his arrival with derision. It was the last time I saw him alive.

My journey back to Derby was lengthy, boring and smelly. It was Ali's socks and truss. I could have kicked myself for deciding to take them home for mother to wash. The Volkswagen Polo stank to high heaven for days afterwards.

Fifty miles from home I decided to ring mother, give her the bad news. The response was typical for her. "Serves them both right for looking at all those half nude young girls," she bellowed. "Too much thinking about sex causes unnecessary deaths." Where was the compassion? Where was the constructive advice for her beleaguered son?

Two bodies lay in Bournemouth mortuary, and all she could do was get aggressive. I resolved to ring Dr.Adcock on my return. A trial spell in the Woody Thickets Home for the Aged suddenly seemed like an excellent idea. Mother needed to rest.

Today's been a rotten day.

I'm sitting in the kitchen watching mother's head spin round and round in the washing machine, wondering what went wrong between us.

Was it the argument over that semolina pudding I wouldn't finish? Was it the horrible leather sandals she bought in Nottingham that I was forced to wear? A man with rabbit teeth doesn't like to be pushed around. I lost control. I'm sorry now. The bread knife I used for the dirty deed snapped in half. Detaching a human head form its body isn't easy. I should have married Wendy Walton when she asked me. I loved her raspberry jam tarts.

Ali seduced the little darling in Markeaton Park when he came to see me last year. I wonder how he did it with a wooden leg?

HOW HE IS

Drunken windbag in a snowstorm
one million miles from
the cosy hearth of his
youth resisting the
advice to stop boozing,
look after his wife and kids.
Someone or something
farts from a nearby
holly bush causing temporary
amusement just before the fears
come.
Then they start to flow, and what a flood,
sobs, and words all in
a blubby muddle
while cackling ghosts from
the cruel school he once
attended pull his ears,
stick filthy sticky fingers up his nose.
There's Cocklington, Barnard
and Bigsby,
Felton, Frame and
old Rickaby,
all plundering his blurred
emotions, creating horrid
drinky winky drunken
mirage after mirage.
But Noreen the naughty
one is never far from
view. "Squeeze his balls
if you can find them"
she will say if pressed.
Good manners and good
fortune where never
companions of hers.
His professed love for her is a
mystery to some.
I just think he's too pissed to care.
Shame old shitty pants,
shame.

LADY LUCK

Lock me in your arms
lady luck, suck my lips
till they pucker all out
of shape.
Boats belch smoke on
the river (it's nineteen fifty two)
as you waltz and wink
with some crappy imaginary
partner.
I'm young - waiting my turn
but a cuddle's all I get
for my lust. I hate it.
I'll be the king of somebody's
heart one day,
I hope.

RAT HEAD

I am burdened with this rat
head of mine,
the whiskers,
the ears with the bright
pink insides.
The rest of me is o.k. though,
I could visit people's houses
and make friends if it wasn't
for my handicap.

ON THE RIVER BANK

Confused, without boots,
barking up the wrong tree,
sublime in my ignorance,
six foot from the river bank.

Once you loved me,
made much of my monkey ears,
called me regularly
from faraway places.

I remember the night you
rang from Bali,
talked of Buster Mathis,
the big fight with Ali.
What the hell did you know about boxing?

Anyway, you should see me now,
in the dusk in pyjamas,
feeling spiritual,
watching the waters for mallard,
yearning to wash the past away.
Did John the Baptist lose his
head for nothing?
Did Singapore let out a collective
howl when the Japs arrived?
I`m at a loss for answers.
Reach me telepathically if possible.

A LITTLE LOVE STORY

There she stood, lovely shadow against the white walls. I heard her laugh and started to weep. It was midnight at midday. I was a romantic fellow but this was too much.

I walked round the room, stared up to the ceiling, shielded a surprise erection with a cupped hand. "It must be love," said a friend later, laughing cynically. But there was more - more than just the stiffening of bone and gristle. I worshipped her with the heart of a million men.

"You're my teddy," she said one day over brunch. I watched her mouth say it, reached for it with my fingers. "Get off," she shouted. I noticed the nicotine stains on her teeth... Little globules I thought, inventing a nasty new word.

I dwelt on her image when she left me, dwelt and dwelt and dwelt. I suffered the hurt of her many affairs with a noble sanctimonious over-indulged heart. Each Saturday I thought of our walks by the river, of her long legs and clumps of stinging nettles: I was stung. "How do I get her back?" I asked a portly drunkard one day in a bar. Stop drinking," came the rapid answer: I did.

Now she's here, long arms dangling over my shoulders as I write. "Kiss the pillow," she's saying (although she lives over the river we often communicate by telepathy) - I'm about to obey. My guardian angel have been good to me and I'm not too proud to admit it. The little globules have turned to a snowy white: the red blood of passion to oceanic blue.

A WRITER'S LOT

In an attempt to write another major work he found himself writing about a collapsible ferret, a biting creature with clockwork claws. "Where do these mad ideas come from?" asked the man in the next bed (he was in hospital for a minor operation at the time). He couldn't think of a suitable answer.
Back at home he continued, this time with a concrete poem in praise of Germany and the German people. "It's very long," whispered his wife as she passed with her lover. He started to cry but gave up after he'd made some scrambled eggs: The World Cup was on television.

In his forty-fifth year he obtained a quickie divorce and married an illiterate seamstress from Central Europe. It's all the fashion here he told his mother on the telephone.
His literary ambitions remained. At the age of forty-seven he started a series of epic plays about the life and times of three Serbian peasants. On completion he presented the manuscripts to his young wife. She blushed. In his fiftieth year he discovered complete happiness when twenty-six of his shorter poems were published in a chic magazine. He was lionized for two weeks, sufficient to keep him content for the final twenty-two years of his life. His young wife was devoted to him seeing true innocence in his cherubic smile and total futility and silliness in his occasional rages. "I'm not a feminist," she said one day in the garden. "Why not!" he demanded determined (as ever) to support every current fad and fashion. "Because I don't want to be," she replied fondling his knee with one hand and eating a tomato with the other. "You're a reactionary," he bellowed. "What do you mean?" she asked - puzzled. With this he shook his head so hard his glasses fell into a bowl of soup she'd just prepared. "I give in," he mumbled after a long pause for breath - "Where did you put my newspaper?"

GETTING BETTER

He sat down to write... "In the midst of the hallucination of time a steamroller squashed his violet pumps." He was Oscar Wilde - or was he? He'd been mad once (or was it twice?) and the thoughts of entering that screaming dark world again shocked him. He decided he wasn't Oscar Wilde; that he was really himself writing about Oscar Wilde. He felt better.

Some days later he was carrying a heavy parcel to the post-office when he was stopped by a woman with piercing brown eyes. "I'm Maria Callas," she said. He paused for a few seconds then called a policeman. "Fetch a doctor!" he shouted - "she's not well." Later he regretted his decision. What if she was Maria Callas? She's dead he thought, and felt relieved. Madness was for other people.

The months passed and the days were sweet. The rancid smell of tortured mind passed through his ears and nose and drifted into clear air. His eyesight seemed sharper (was it the new reading glasses?) and existence seemed worth the existing. "I'm well," he called to a passing sparrow and then added sadly... "but I can't fly." This great truth resounded through his considerable cranium, his vanity truly exposed. "Time for tea," called a voice from the direction of the French windows. He stood - rigid - softened - then turned to walk indoors.

DARK INTO LIGHT

Damaged again
sitting at the water's edge
trousers on fire

purple light
moon and stars
dogs and dogs

whistling ghosts
somewhere at my back
boredom at my back

close to a heaven
but how far?
Who cares
The energy to smile returns.

A PERFECT SUNDAY

Zen at the weekend

two cups, a sausage
a shadow on his toupee

"Is this it?" he asks
the cat

LOVE STORY WITH AUTHOR'S NOTE

To all intents and purposes he was the great lover - king of the village. The reality however was somewhat different. At nights he was beset by nightmares about flying golf balls and invaders from strange suburban planets. There were times when he woke in a hot sweat and thought he was Norwegian: Lapland beckoned at every turn. Mondays were terrible. Still - what did it matter? His myth hummed through every dinner party - he was talked about.

One freezing winter he was ironing tea towels when the headmistress from the local girl's school knocked on the door. It was love at first sight - a sweet combination of reward and punishment. They both compared themselves to little pots of yogurt (much to the surprise of their friends). There was an intimate rapport.

And then there was the other love - the similar love - the equal love...How was she? She was his river, fast and furious but never treacherous... But the hum of dissent continued and the villagers prattled until the arrival of an angel disguised as a Swedish sea captain.
AUTHOR'S NOTE: It was late at night when I wrote this piece and a little brainstorm caused me to lose track of the sense of it all. I was forced (with reluctance) to abandon the trivia and fall into the arms of my lover. As I did so my busy pen fell to the floor drawing blood from the naked foot in passing.
"Ouch," I cried. "Young man," she said, "make haste with your pursuit, all this scribbling has left me wanting." As I kissed her full rich lips I paused: Why was she using such a strange archaic tongue? It was a fleeting thought, soon forgotten in the hurly-burly of love play.

TO A SIBLING

Two frogs and a paper napkin
seven dwarfs
and a melting portrait of
Walt Disney

Salvador Dali in a wheelchair
directing the London Symphony Orchestra
in a performance
of some old Spanish rubbish

Imagery rampant
Imagery rampant
but meaning Nil.
Art for Arthur's sake?
Why not!

THIS PIECE IS FOR MY BROTHER

HEADS

We often exchange heads. I would say I prefer mine to hers. It's the hairstyle, the earrings, the silver lipstick. I don't feel right when I go to the pub for my nightcap. Some of the locals don't like it either. Barry Bingham, my best friend when I'm wearing my own head, always refuses to talk to me. It's hurtful.
A few nights ago, she said she wanted to stop exchanging heads for a while, "have a rest, learn to enjoy looking at my own face in the bathroom mirror for a week or two," as she put it. I told her I liked the idea, that swopping heads was sometimes a source of distress for me. "Me too," she said, "that Pakistani greengrocer always starts giggling when I've got your head on. It'll be a relief to have a break." As we chatted, a surly baboon stared at us through the living room window. "They're everywhere these days," commented my wife. "I hear Jack Parker's mother has persuaded one of them to do her garden this summer."
The week before last it had been wild pigs, dozens and dozens of them. Our local cinema was sold out completely for three nights in a row. Pigs love Walt Disney productions. Our youngest was particularly annoyed. "They get more pocket money than us," she moaned. "I'm lucky to go to the movies once a month with the measly amount you hand out." It was the same when a herd of Jersey cows decided to organise a football match on one of the city parks.
"Why have they got proper goalposts when we have to make do with a pile of coats?" was the first question a nephew of ours asked after witnessing an exciting 2 – 2 draw. I was lost for an answer. Their football boots were a bit of a mystery too. Where they real leather or just cheap plastic? And who made their colourful shirts and shorts? Life gets more confusing as I get older. Two days ago I went to the office in pyjamas and slippers, got drunk on a bottle of vodka during the afternoon break, then threw my boss down a flight of stairs for a five- pound bet.
I haven't got the sack yet, although I'm expecting something nasty in the post any day now. "If you had been wearing my head this nonsense wouldn't have happened," said my wife jokingly at breakfast today. Our miniature poodle Eric started laughing fit to bust. I felt like hitting him over the head with the coffee pot. Flippancy isn't required when one's financial future is in doubt. A dog should know its place at all times, even if he speaks three languages and plays excellent banjo. I'm all for

animals participating in our human lives but I draw the line at insensitivity in any creature. I think I'll take him into the back yard and shoot him at the weekend.

2

I tried head swopping with my eldest son once. It didn't work out. I developed spots all over my chest, feet and private parts. Randy, that's the name his mother gave him – I hate it, almost choked on his cheeseburger when I told him. "It's that stupid, foul smelling hair cream you've sloshed all over my head," he spluttered, starting to yelp like a demented rabid hound.
"I either get spots or a permanent erection if I as much as get a whiff of it. Wash my hair out, at once!" I did as he bid me with great haste. It was disturbing to watch my own face distort itself horribly into something somewhere between rage and hurt confusion. Handing him his head back, washed, combed and free of all creams, was a great relief. We never tried the experiment again.
My youngest daughter, to my great chagrin, has recently starting asking, and I blame myself for this, to "swap heads with Daddy."
Now the idea of striding round town with a seven year old's head (with pigtails) on my on broad shoulders strikes me as very odd indeed. I refuse to even consider her request. I'm sure I'd have some tweedy miss from the childcare department on my back if I as much as gave her crackpot idea a second thought. I can't cope with officialdom. My father was the same. He once cut a traffic warden's ear off with a pair of scissors after she'd given him a parking ticket. He kept it in a shoebox under his bed until he passed away. We were a happy family. Mother, I can still see that toothless grin of hers as I write, kept some of the most intelligent chickens in the U.K. Three of them played the accordions and won prizes all over the place. Another flew to Australia and back in just under two years. His prize was a small Christmas pudding. I don't know why he bothered.

3

Exchanging ones head for that of a friend or relative is no longer a favourite thing to do. The activity reached its peak of popularity in the swinging sixties. Yes, I remember Carnaby Street in London buzzing from end to end with head changers, Trafalgar Square's pigeons shitting mercilessly on my wife's new hairdo after I'd borrowed her considerable cranium for the afternoon. Sad. It's all petered out to nothing now. Our little family is probably the last active group of head swoppers on this beautiful island of ours, and our enthusiasm's fading fast. I've heard the cats and dogs aren't doing it as much as they used to either. Eric the poodle used to regularly exchange with Mandy the corgi from next door until about a year ago. I'm not sure what went wrong with the arrangement. My wife thinks Eric got annoyed because Mandy tried an experimental swap with a piglet from Dashwood's farm. I haven't inquired too deeply though. Eric tends to savage the settee if pressed about private matters. I understand. I once decapitated a neighbour's Amazonian parrot for staring down my wife's low cut blouse and saying "beautiful bobbly gazoomas" over and over again.

Extreme sensitivity runs in my family. Dad once threw a soft-boiled egg at an elderly member of the royal family because he thought, mistakenly, that the Queen wanted to persuade parliament to ban head swapping in public parks. I remember visiting him in prison afterwards and being forcibly restrained from exchanging heads. My childish rage caused me to urinate but Mum, ever the rock, wiped it up with my school cap before any of the authorities noticed.

I've been discussing my likely loss of regular work with some of my colleagues. The general opinion seems to be that my boss, when he returns from hospital, will keep me on.

"He's a good Christian," said the chief accountant when I asked his opinion on the matter.

"Chaps like him are forced to forgive. It'll be O.K."

I'm not so sure. His Siamese cat keeps ringing me up threatening to claw my eyes out, do a big poo on my rose bushes and terrorise Eric the poodle into exchanging heads. Clouds are gathering over our peaceful home. A bunch of wild pigs have been uttering obscenities through the letter-box for much of this afternoon. My boss has contacts everywhere. Something awful could easily happen. Eric wants to borrow my head and shout at the pigs through the bay window. He's going nuts. I must take him out for a good long walk, if this all passes over.

ENCYCLOPEDIA
A. B. C. D.

A

ALBANIA

Albania, I dream of you, Enver Hoxha sitting shitting on a dirty yellow plastic piss pot. Then there's Tirana, bruised old Tirana (population 243,000), the chain-smoking student in the anorak I met in a nightmare. "It's a Hoxha's fat arse," he croaked, "he sits like a brain starved whale on us all." I handed him a limp lettuce, a big fat bag of my father's best tomatoes. He took them and threw them into the dust. "It's a goat I require," he snapped, pointedly, as the blood of revolutions spurted from the sudden crack in his head. Stone faced Enver, are you happy now? I give you this anorak as a present.

ANGST

It was the fish I fried to eat eating back, the tiny teeth sucking at the crown of my head as we wrestled, hungry. I was afraid, so he won. That summer night I took him to my favourite, pebbled Cornish beach in my Donald Duck sandcastle-making bucket. He laughed (how pretentious this all sounds) as I flung him back into the sea. Mummy made me lace up her corsets when I got back to the holiday bungalow. Daddy made some pungent cheese sandwiches.

PAUL ANKA

One day I heard two variety agents shouting excitedly to each other over the telephone. Here's the gist of the conversation.

First agent: Paul Anka's his name. This kid has got it. Pipes of solid gold!

SECOND AGENT: Got what? A head the size of the forbidden planet, eyes that cajole one to dance on top of the ice box for no particular reason; fulsome lips that remind

	one that paradise is just at the end of the avenue? What? What are you talking about? What are pipes?
First Agent:	Vocal chords, you Serbian son of back street watchmaker: loud, lustrous, commercially viable vocal chords. Must I shout? Must I always put myself in this aggressive role? I'm a gentle old soul when it comes down to it.
Second agent:	Give me a break. You're as gentle as a cutting wind across a desolate arctic wasteland. Anyway, why all the fuss? What's so super special about this artiste you're trying to sell me?
First Agent:	Simple answer: talent, teen appeal; a face that makes the little girls want to weep. He's written a song called "Diana" that frequently causes my fourteen year old niece to wet the bed.
Second agent:	Wow! That's really something. Is she called Diana by any chance? Does she think it's written for her?
First agent:	I've no idea. All I know he's got the pipes to make us all millionaires. Interested?

ANOREXIA

It was hard watching Katie disappear. Colin, who, when asked, would say he loved her more than words can describe, sometimes found temporary solace in the company of drunken friends. It was a dead end. All the alcohol in the world wouldn't shift Katie from the settee; make her constantly prostrate stick-like form strong and well again. She was fit for nothing useful. The house was a morgue. When she asked: "Am I beautiful?" his eyes would drip tears. "Who is this frail insect?" he would ask himself, and irritation, hate, total love would mingle momentarily in his mind, crease up his forehead into a troubled frown. Then things changed. Katie started eating again while watching a Laurel and Hardy film on T.V. "I'll be happy, fat and very endearing," she chirped brightly after she'd finished her first hamburger in months.

"Oliver Hardy will be my guiding light from now on. I want to be flabby and funny." Colin put it down to a miracle, although he secretly shuddered at the prospect of having a mirthful, overweight wife in the house. Had he been praying too hard to the wrong god, a distant deity with a cruel sense of humour? The ups and downs of fate would be forever a mystery. A wife that he had confidently thought would vanish was about to reappear. It was time to stock up the fridge. His shrunken shadow of a spouse was up and alive and hungry again.

ARAB

The clock spins round to Arab time. Jack promptly dons his white cloak (made from the very best of silk curtain material), squeezes his homemade pink pillbox hat on his head, runs into the street shouting, "Come hither bold Socrates, make haste to my house for we've work to do." The strangeness of his attire causes comment from a passer-by. The damning words "silly bugger" can be heard clearly above the noise of lawnmowers. Suburbia doesn't want Jack. The sight of a retired librarian dressed Arab style "lowers the tone." House prices could fall to horrific depths.

When "bold Socrates" doesn't arrive, Jack races indoors to order a taxi. Beryl, his wheelchair bound sister, starts shouting hysterically, grabs a small pistol from the cutlery drawer. She fires three times. Jack falls down, dead.

All lawnmowers cease moving. A summery Sunday kind of silence takes over. Socrates, the friendliest and most loyal of camels, finally arrives. "Am I too late?" he inquires, poking a lovable lumpy head through the kitchen window. Beryl laughs nervously, points to Jack's crumpled form. "Just a little," she says, taking the gun from her pinafore pocket, aiming carefully at the camel's long neck.

ADOLF

Our eldest son was born with a moustache, so we called him Adolf. He always hated the name. Oh the arguments we had. The air was blue with bad language sometimes. He moved away four Septembers ago, moved to Rostock, changed from Adolf to Jens. Jens doesn't sound right to me. Why didn't he pick something a bit more traditional? Josef, for instance. Heinrich? Anyway, what's wrong with Adolf? A baby born with a moustache should always be called Adolf. Our son's ungrateful. He was forever complaining about being laughed at when he was school, completely oblivious to the suffering his mother went through. How did he think she felt when the midwife presented her with a moustached baby? Everyone in the hospital was laughing. She was under sedation for days afterwards. As far as I'm concerned he can rot in Rostock forever. Let's face it; he didn't have to push himself around in a pushchair with all the neighbours pointing. I detested taking him for a walk in the park. It's strange, there were paranoid moments when I thought even the birds were tittering. And the doctors weren't much help, either. My pleas for something to remove the moustache permanently fell on unsympathetic ears. All they could suggest was regular shaving. It was so frustrating, so utterly shaming. Adolf's our only child. We didn't dare risk another. The image of a little girl with a moustache has been haunting my mind, before sleep, for years now.

B

BAVARIA

Hell could be those leather shorts they wear in Bavaria. I consider them to be insufferable apparel in the middle of a cruel cold winter, pure torture when worn too tight on a hot summer's day. My pen friend in Munich considers me extremely odd, says my fears concerning the garment are an example of "typical English stupidity" and "bloody silly." I resent his obnoxious attitude; refuse to accept such boneheaded bigotry. The man lacks a clear overview. Misguided patriotic fervour is rife in his part of the world. Bavaria interests me though. My pen friend, who's forever scribbling on about the scenic wonders of the place, has suggested I visit him. I think it's a plot. I'm sure he and his blond haired, ruddy cheeked friends are planning to trap me in the corner of a beer garden, force me to a wear a pair of excessively small leather shorts. The stress to my balls could cause terminal damage. I'm about to get married. I don't think I'll go.

BRITISH

"You are from Britain?" she asked. "Yes," I replied, "And you know Bognor Regis?" she asked. "No," I replied tersely. We were sitting on Stockholm railway station waiting for a train. She was a complete stranger: Swedish, plump, mildly aggressive, stunningly dull. I was travelling the world looking for fun, but visiting Sweden had been a big mistake. My search for drunken parties, erotic encounters in lowlife bars, mysterious liaisons in back street hotels, was a flop. Nagging irritation soured my mood. She continued: "Is the Yorkshire pudding a necessity at every Sunday dinner? Can Exeter be reached by bicycle from London?" I closed my eyes, prayed for patience. A decrepit old pigeon pecked furiously round my shoes. My train was late. The world, so often a rich source of merriment, had become grey, blank, Swedish. She wouldn't stop: "Is Margaret Thatcher someone you admire? Do women drive buses in the great British cities? How do you boil your cabbage?" It went on and on and on. Then I exploded. "Fuck off," I roared, aiming a kick at my sturdy rucksack, mentally cursing the Union Jack I'd misguidedly sown on it. "Can't you see I want to be left alone?" There was a short silence as we both stared hard at the persistent pigeon. I got up to walk to another seat. "Don't you like your great nation?" I heard her say, voice as shrill and sure as ever. "Don't you eat Christmas pudding on Christmas day?" Nothing short of throwing her on the railway track in front of an advancing train would stop her talking. I banished the nasty thought from my brain. "No," I said, "never, never, never."

BANANAS

I once met a fat old man on a park bench in the English seaside town of Bournemouth. It was mid afternoon. A shimmering summer sea filled the distance horizon. We talked about bananas. I have no idea why. Later, for no particular reason, I jotted down some of the things that were said. The following transcription is a fragment:

ME: God bless our old friend the banana. I hear tell it's the only fattening fruit.

HIM: This is correct. A man in Manchester ate six of the things every morning and died of a heart attack at a football match. I read there were some who said his face turned bright yellow, that his ankles were green.

ME: Green ankles? Wasn't he wearing socks?

HIM: I've no earthly idea. Sufficient to say it was the bananas that did it. Socks or no socks he was dead as dead can be when he arrived at the hospital.

ME: What a tragedy. My experience with the fruit has been nothing but positive. I love to slice the blighter up and toss it over my cornflakes. It's the perfect start to a working day.

HIM: Don't you feel sick when you ride on the top deck of the bus to work?

ME: No. My office is very close to my home. I walk.

HIM: A fitness fanatic, eh? The kind of man who does press ups in the bathroom, before he takes the plunge?

ME: Not true. I just happen to love bananas. Life without my favourite fruit would be a sea of half-eaten apple cores, a landscape strewn with rejected, squashed strawberries. The banana is my health-giving friend. I prefer its taste to almost anything.

HIM: Spoken like a true devotee. Our cricketing friends in Jamaica must be proud of you.

ME: Why?

HIM: Your preference for one of their leading crops has to make you a hero of theirs.

ME: But I don't know any Jamaicans.

HIM: Perhaps not. However, if you did, I'm sure you'd be their first choice to drink a rum with.

BRIDE

She lives in the vicarage midst dangerous, dusty cacti, a hat that's a cardboard castle plopped on top of her curls. Simon Bradshaw, smitten to the core of his piggy baby balls, would woo her if he could, probably molest her, mount her, marry her. Sadly, poor Simon hasn't a hope. As a former boy scout, a beaming, baying, forever jolly type with a distinct bald patch, he should begin to pay heed to reality. Daughters of priests (for his dream girl's father cares for the souls of the parish faithful) can be notoriously choosy, often seeking marital partners with a pronounced stoop and an inbred capacity for melancholy. I write, unfortunately, from experience. How could I ever forget Marlene Trotter, dimple cheeked mistress of my mind and overfed body? Wasn't it I who contemplated suicide as the only solution to her constant rebuffs? And wasn't she, too, the daughter of a cleric? Simon Bradshaw could be me as I was and am. His long vigils in the rain outside the vicarage gates (endured in the hopes of seeing that focus of his all) only serve to remind me of my foolishness. Some kind friend should tell him the truth, persuade him that he and our kind are not meant to tarry with the daughters of vicars. I know. I'm a wreck because I tried. The happy go lucky personality I once possessed is now a memory. Vicious hate can supplant true love. My story this last seven years is proof of it. Only last night I stood outside Marlene's house, gazed up in torment at her bedroom window, imagined my beloved and that bespectacled, bookish fool she married fucking in the dark. I worry about myself sometimes. My search for a bride still goes on, though. I won't give in. I can't.

BASTARD

Dennis is a bastard because he won't let Tracy ride on his mountain bike. Every weekend she sobs about it. "Bastard," she says, loud enough for anybody passing to hear. I don't like it. Girls shouldn't use bad language. My father believes that the female who swears is no better than a prostitute. I fully agree with him. He was a policeman when younger and knows about these things. Dennis can be a bastard when he likes. There have been quite a few times when his habit of exposing himself to all and sundry has made me venomously angry. I spat in his face last time he did it. "Nobody wants to see your balls on this housing estate," I shouted. He's immature for a twelve year old. There are people of his age who are already responsible enough to work in supermarkets.

Tracy once offered to pull her jeans down and show Dennis everything in exchange for a ride on his bike. The stupid bastard refused. I could have smacked him. I've always liked looking at female private parts. Still, Dennis will always be Dennis. The personality we develop early on usually sticks with us forever. My father still wears his old policeman's uniform when he digs the garden.

BEANS

Two young women were talking about their boyfriends on a tram in Nürnberg. I couldn't help overhearing:

FIRST WOMAN: Does your boyfriend like beans? Mine does. He farts like a hurricane in bed. The neighbours knocked on the wall last night.

SECOND WOMAN: Why? Was your television on too loud? Was the dog barking?

FIRST WOMAN: No. It was him breaking wind. He'd just eaten a whopping great Mexican salad with beans. I told him not to do it.

SECOND WOMAN: But perhaps he couldn't help it? Beans are delicious but treacherous. I had them a lot last time we were in Portugal.

FIRST WOMAN: Portugal! I've been there. I slept with a Chinese boy in a tent. It was really romantic; the first time and only time I ever did it with someone from Hong Kong. We were on the beach. I think I lost my sunglasses.

SECOND WOMAN: Did you tell your boyfriend you did it? Was he on holiday with you at the time? Mine's very very jealous. He'd take a whip to my naked arse if he caught me fooling around.

FIRST WOMAN: How perverse. And you'd let him do it?

SECOND WOMAN: Yes. I believe a woman should be punished hard if she double-crosses the man in her life. I like a man to be a man.
Mine farts whenever he feels like it. He loves his beans, like yours.

FIRST WOMAN: Interesting. Do you feel free to fart when the feeling comes over you?

SECOND WOMAN: Certainly not. A true lady fights off her urges, keeps everything in. I'm extremely good at it. I've never made a noise or smell in public in my life.

FIRST WOMAN: Oh dear. Suddenly I have a mental picture of you controlling yourself, going purple in the face and getting dizzy. I feel sorry for you.

SECOND WOMAN: Don't. I consider myself to be lucky in life. I sleep with a man amongst boys. Pooh! I can smell his farts now.

FIRST WOMAN: And you like them?

SECOND WOMAN: Sort of. They're a whiff of him being him, I suppose.

C

CHOLERA

Did the sea captain novelist, Joseph Conrad (real name Theodore Korzeniowski) ever dream of cholera? Did he sometimes wake from a jungle of a nightmare with the words "terminal diarrhoea" on his lips? Cholera is a killer disease, a lurking horror for those unfortunates who happen to dwell in tropical climes. Conrad must have been trembling in his sea boots every time he visited Africa. I'm sure he was heard to say "Lord save me from the clutch of cholera" when called upon to hobnob with some great chief. "Lord Jim," I'm told, is one of his best novels. I'm a big reader, but I haven't read it yet. The old concentration isn't always what it should be.

My girlfriend Rachel (bless her kinky little patent leather pumps) recently raced through everything Conrad ever wrote. I have a great regard for her enthusiasm. Cholera, however, hounds us both. We think we might have it. Can you catch it from library books?

CHRIST

Christ came to me one cold night last April. "What is it you require?" I asked in my best English. "Is the damp in the forest too much for you?" The saviour of us all shook his head. "It's your soul I've come for," he said, smiling the most impossibly beautiful smile. It's available and I want it." "But you already have it," I protested. "The Pope in Rome's got all the necessary information." Christ scowled, tugged hard at his beard with long nervous fingers. "That fool in Italy is an upstart," he snapped, "makes Christians out of everybody whether I approve or not." There was a sudden distant roar of thunder as he spoke; mice skipped about under the floorboards. Nature verified his greatness in no uncertain fashion.

"What should I do then?" I stammered, sitting stiffly up in bed to demonstrate my eagerness to please. "Go downstairs and make me a nice cup of cocoa," he said, flashing a smile, "and we'll talk about it." I leapt out of bed immediately. When I returned with the cocoa he was gone. A hastily written note lay on the bedside table. "Thanks for the drink," it said, "but a pressing matter with a sinner from the next village needs to be attended to. Can you forgive me? I know your cocoa's very good." "How kind of him," I thought, sipping the hot drink, while rain beat a heavy tattoo on my bedroom window. Then a warm, indescribably secure feeling filled my body from head to toe. "You have my soul," I said, aloud, without really knowing why. "I can feel it."

There was shrieking childish laughter from under the bed. "It's just the cocoa," murmured a voice, not unlike his from somewhere beyond the bedroom door. I slept badly. Mother chastised me for using all the milk up when I got down to breakfast.

COUCH

Fattybody Henry sleeps on the couch, eats on the couch, fornicates supremely badly on the couch. Plump but petite Pandora ("You'll adore me when you get to know me" is one of her favourite sayings) perches precariously on a rickety chair close by. A life of squalor, unfortunately, would seem to be their lot. Henry hasn't worked for more than seven years. Pandora ("such sweet eyes when she's crying," said a friend) has been the victim of a cripplingly mysterious backache for over four. Ah if only life were a mite kinder. Oh if only they'd passed the necessary examinations and become world famous surgeons. When Henry is heard to say, "I was born for this couch," he's simply giving voice to a deeply held conviction that has placed him firmly in the forefront of life's extreme under achievers for years. And Pandora? She's the willing ally, a preening but docile blob of collusion. They are the perfect match.

COVENTRY

There are lights in the sky over the city of Coventry tonight. But who is awake to see them? They go to bed early in this part of England, fuck and ferret about under blankets without ever a thought of mysterious things. It's a rotten shame. If Jesus himself was to make a nightly visit to their much vaunted new cathedral they would be sure to be otherwise engaged. A workmate of mine once said that no one in Coventry would give a bugger if King Farouk did a striptease in Woolworth's. I've often thought it might be interesting to put his theory to the test (if the monarch in question was still alive, though it's hard to imagine the chubbiest king Egypt ever had naked amidst rows of cheap saucepans making a complete fool of himself). I had a girlfriend from Coventry once. She was boring, always talking about the Second World War and how much she hated Germany ("They almost bombed us into oblivion" was something she said far too frequently). I left her crying at the bus station in Derby some eleven years ago. I haven't seen or heard of her since.

COMPUTER

He has no computer, just a sturdy leather-bound notepad and sock full of pencil stubs. They that say they know say a computer should be a constant companion, talk of it as if to be without one is foolish to the extreme. What piffle! The heart of an angel is contained in the soul of man. Can a computer boast of such a thing? Can a computer boast at all? It's just a plastic information centre with a brain borrowed from a droning team of pessimistic scientists. He that's without is fortunate without a doubt. God bless his notepad, his stubby little pencils. I am, maybe, a backward looking type (Was that a sneer I saw on your lips just now?) but I'm happy with it. He that craves a computer will a computer become. He that is without computer will busy himself with thoughts of God and heaven more frequently.

COUSIN

My cousin has red hair, an arse that juts out prominently when he straightens his back. My cousin was married but is now divorced. My cousin wanted to be a professional footballer. My cousin is a clerical assistant in an office full of screaming, abusive feminists. My cousin (on my mother's side) drinks far too much, frequents striptease joints at the weekends. My cousin lives in a one bedroomed flat with a Nigerian family for neighbours. My cousin is a racist. My cousin is a man of few words. My cousin sulks. My cousin masturbates. My cousin only smiles when Chelsea F.C. are having a good season. I don't like my cousin.

D

DIARRHOEA

This is what I heard through the bedroom wall when I was a child. I think I was ten years old.

Mum: Has a rat got into the room?

Dad: No. It's nothing but the odour of the night, a sour echo of a misspent day. Ignore it, take your rest, close those still girlish eyes of yours. Have you taken your sleeping pills?

Mum: I've not, and I won't. You know they make me dizzy when I'm cooking your breakfast.
I like to have my wits about me when I'm frying sausages.

Dad: Perhaps you should reduce the dose? Have you spoken to Doctor Flynn?

Mum: That Flynn is a dirty old man, always inspecting my nipples for no reason at all. They tell me he pulled his housekeeper's pants down once when she was peeling potatoes. He's got no respect for womankind.

Dad: Was that you or a passing motorbike? I've never heard such a noise. Could it be that
spicy fiddle faddle you cooked for dinner? I like my food plain and simple, haricot beans to be haricot beans.

Mum: Why have you changed the subject? I was talking about Doctor Flynn and his filthy turn of mind. What's the matter? Does the truth about our friendly family doctor offend you? My God, for a man who loves his oats as much as you do you've a very puritanical streak.

Dad: You broke wind. Why can't you admit it? I've got the same problem. I've had diarrhoea for most of this evening.

Mum: You swine. I pour out my problems and all you can talk about is shitting yourself. Is there a rat in the room?

Dad: Of course not. We need some of God's good air in here. I'll open the window.

DIPLOMA

Neville hasn't got a diploma. Carol, who says she loves him more than words can possibly describe, wishes he had. The lack of this all-important document is a barrier. Neville sulks when mention is made of it, whispers things like "Einstein wasn't very good at school either" to ease his shame. Carol suggests night classes. Neville gets cross each time she mentions them. Existence, for Neville, must be experienced without qualifications. "Blessed are the ignorant," he's often heard muttering after one of Carol's gentle verbal attacks, "for it is they that do the donkey work in this world." Carol would marry Neville if she thought he could provide for her properly; earn sufficient cash each month to enable her to be regularly pampered at fashionable beauty salons. Sadly, Neville just laughs the subject off when she brings it up. "A good strip wash at the kitchen sink" is his idea of luxury. There are those on this earth who denounce all yearning for the good life as decadent and sinful. I, in all truth, cannot be counted amongst them. Carol has my sympathy and admiration. When the moment is ripe I'll offer this beauteous secretary of mine my hand in marriage. Neville, of course, will have to be somehow cajoled into agreeing. I'm confident, however, of the outcome. My position in this firm gives me the power to offer him a job, with pension, in the mail order department. I'm sure he'll agree to drop all claims to Carol when I suggest the idea. After all, his current job as garbage collector for the city council must only be confirming his sense of total failure.

DOCTOR

Would that my doctor could perform plastic surgery, could turn this mish mash of a face of mine into a thing to be drooled over. "Silly Kevin," he said when I suggested, half jokingly, he try. Then he sent me to a psychiatrist colleague of his for a thorough check-up. Nothing was resolved. Nothing is now. The determination to alter this facial disaster of mine for the better remains stronger than ever. "The gates of heaven are only open to those that smile nicely" was something my mother said, with a regularity that bordered on obsession. I would like to satisfy all requirements for entrance. My smile, at the moment, is a complete abomination. No wonder small children pull their pullovers over their heads when I pass by. Mother nature should be ashamed of herself. There is some hope, though. A neighbour of mine has a cousin whose husband is a noted plastic surgeon, a man who, to avoid tax, has been know to perform operations at a reduced rate. I must give him a ring. Walking round town has become a trial of patience lately. How many more times do I have to hear people calling me "ugly mush," before I slap them in the mouth? My doctor is a prize arsehole, a man lacking both sensitivity and commonsense. I'm the monster of the community and all he can do is send me to some half-wit psychiatrist. There has to be some action. As I write this I can feel the fingers on my left hand growing longer and longer and longer. Oh God, another deformity to live with, another cruel blow to my self-esteem? There's a storm on outside. The tree my father planted twenty years before he died is bending fit to break. Will that big parrot that sits on top of it each evening survive? I'm concerned. I think I'll call the fire service.

DIAMONDS

"Fart in the face of adversity," she said, "think diamonds and expensive hotels and poodles wearing velveteen bonnets." He hadn't the imagination to comply with her suggestion, as it was as much as he could manage to boil himself an egg in the morning. The difficult business of surviving was all. Concentration was required. But she persisted: "Dance with naked damsels in your dreams. Flummox the devil with songs of hope. Tie a yellow ribbon round your penis before retiring for the night." The optimism of it all sounded almost inviting, though the cruel realities of his physical self (one arm, one leg, a nose the size of a well nurtured carrot) prevented him from showing any trace of genuine enthusiasm. To be grumpy and self-pitying was to be his fate in life. Was it the motorbike accident, a horror from which he'd only partially recovered, that ensured this? She was the diamond type. He, before his tragic joust with danger, was little more than a layabout and sponger: all beer, skittles, humping fair maidens in pub yards. Her devotion, though admirable, confused her friends. Wasn't she the child of wealthy, devoted parents? Hadn't she attended the very best private schools? A wise man (or was it a woman?) once said, "Love is the strangest thing of all." True or false? Maybe the stars that shine like diamonds over their humble dwelling bear witness to some magnificent mystery?

DENMARK

Deborah writes frequently to her pen friend in America. Here's a typical example of her fanciful, forthright, amusing style.

Dear Cindy,

Did you know I was a Viking's woman in another life and lived in Denmark? It was awful. I had only one dress and one pair of knickers. Winter was a nightmare. The snow was so deep it used to bury our piglets. Bodo, the man I was forced to live with by my drunken stepfather, wasn't much use ("A carbuncle on the sweet face of nature," my mummy used to call him) and spent most of his time sleeping with the sheep in the barn. One day I took one of his swords and stabbed him through the heart. They burnt me as a witch afterwards.

I'm always having flashbacks. Last week I was making a cup of tea and suddenly saw myself selling mushrooms to Hans Christian Andersen in a Copenhagen vegetable shop. Cindy oh Cindy, he had the sweetest, kindest face I've ever seen on a man. I wanted to take him home, cuddle him, and bake one of my special raspberry cakes. I guess you could say it was instant rapport. Have you ever been to Denmark? I haven't – yet. Daddy, who's more than a little Nordic in features, says we might be going next year. I come all over hot when I think about it. What if I should bump into the ghost of Bodo in those Tivoli Gardens? Would he give me a good thumping and drag me by my hair back to his hut? Perhaps I'm scaring myself unnecessarily? Mummy says Danes are peace loving these days. I'm sure she's right. Have you read any stories by Hans Christian Andersen? Do you know that one about the little mermaid? I must close now, as Daddy's just asked me to take the dog out for a walk. I'll write again soon.

Kind regards to your parents

Deborah

P.S. Have you got President Clinton's autograph yet?

DYNAMITE

Her love is dynamite, doth kindle fiery rhythms in my, normally, unmusical brain. Tra la la la la la loo I go, bongoing upon saucepans and such. "It's a shame to see him like this," say some, "when we know, in all probability, he's a damned sight more intelligent than most." What condescending nonsense they speak. I love being slightly askew. Why, only yesterday, I spoke to a sparrow in the backyard about my passion and he trilled and trilled for joy. My surly slob of a flatmate made comments on the performance later, said nasty things like, "Why didn't you stuff some breadcrumbs down its beak and choke it to death?" How was I to know the fool was trying to sleep? Dynamite love (and the rhapsody in one it encourages) doesn't suit everyone's frame of mind. Celibate priests, for instance, positively discourage it; while well-groomed Buddhists turn pink, make flapping movements with their arms. Dynamite is always dynamite. Frogs, at least those that slither and slide about my private parts, are nearly always green. Ahoy for love, I say. Pass me the oars, let me row cross her bathtub full of bloody rags. My dream is to kiss her (whoever she is) till our mouths begin to bleed.

JIM AND LYDIA CHEW THE FAT

Jim?

Yes?

The confusion I felt when the balloon went up remains a permanent fixture in this thicket I call a mind. Jason hadn't a clue what he was about to unleash when he let that young fellow with Slavic cheekbones run around the cemetery with a chain saw. Three headless pensioners where removed to the city morgue; a bull terrier was chopped in half.

How do know they were pensioners, Lydia?

It was the headscarves and zip up fur bootees. I think I recognised an overcoat I presented to the church jumble sale last year.
All positive clues, Jim. There's a little bit of the Miss Marple in me somewhere. Fred often says I would have made a wonderful policewoman. I once caught a cat burglar, locked him in the coal shed.

Remarkable. And was he wearing a blue knitted hat, sporting a large red beard? Did he call himself Tarzan when the police arrested him? Oh this constipation, these warts on my left forefinger. I've been scratching my arse for days for no reason at all.

Have you been to see a doctor?
You go camping a lot don't you? Something could have got into your socks and trousers – fleas, termites, moths, earthworms...anything. I once knew a man who went camping and woke up with a frog sitting on his chin. Did you pitch your tent near a pond? Did you rinse your underpants through and spread them over a bush to dry? I've completed a study of human fallibility, made stringent tests with washing powders, liquid stain removers, corseleted uncles, maiden aunts with little hairy dogs that sniff where they shouldn't. It's the beast in us that confounds the normal. Do you sniff cocaine?

Never, ever. I couldn't afford the stuff even if I fancied it. I'm but putty in the hands of the tobacco manufacturers though. A colleague at the

office absconded with my wig at work last week, snatched it from my head and threw it out of a window on to the traffic in the street below. It was a protest against my smoking in the toilet. I struck him down with a fire extinguisher. Wigs are expensive items.
Irate anti-smokers, whatever their status, shouldn't be allowed to make free with them. I would have acted in the same way if the chap had been the archbishop of Canterbury. I won't stand for unfairness.

Neither will the archbishop, Jim.
He's made a profession out of it. It must feel funny trying to constantly appease the nastiness inside, trying to be all things to all men at all times. I couldn't do it. I've always been the explosive one in our house. The Pope in Rome would get a good punching if he caught me in a bad mood at breakfast time. I'm no respecter of persons.

Oh Lydia, I had no idea. How does your Fred cope?

I stick a toasting fork up his arse and pull his nose hard with a big pair of pliers. No, seriously, he manages my little tantrums extremely well. I've lost count of the times he's laced my evening cocoa with night nurse. He's a crafty old devil. The attraction of ripe cheese to so many members of the general public has always been a mystery to me.

Pardon?

The way they sit, sniffing and chewing, passing pertinent comments to each other, nodding and licking their sun parched lips. I've watched them on holiday, squirmed at their olive consumption, forced myself to look away. All those men with Slavic cheekbones. All those half dead pensioners in floral shorts.

Isn't this where we came in: pensioners, men with Slavic cheekbones?

And the bull terrier sliced in half, Jason watching the slaughter with shock and a kind of wonderment flashing across those big blue eyes of his. The balloon went up in no uncertain terms. I personally supervised the padlocking of the cemetery gates, roused the head gardener from his afternoon nap, shared a bottle of wine with him and his harlot of a girlfriend afterwards.

In his hut? Did you drink it in his hut?

No. On a bench, a park bench.

And Jason?

He pooed in his dungarees and went home to change them. I think he'll get the sack when Albert comes back from wherever he's gone to. The cemetery authorities don't take kindly to junior employees who allow Slavic cheeked monsters to run riot on their property. Quite a few graves were trampled on.

Anybody's we know?

Colin Ashburton.

Brother of Cedric, father of Katie Wagstaff? Not that little fat former wrestler and children's entertainer who made us all laugh at Snotty Garfield's wedding?

The very same. All the fancy plant pots were shattered. I could have wept when I swept them up. A nicely turned out grave is a joy to the world. I think it helps us forget the horrors that lie beneath, so to speak. I love flowers in bloom, always have. I'm a glutton for shoe polish on Sunday mornings. How's your mother's swollen ankles? I heard she had troubles getting sneakers to fit her. Does she still enjoy a game of tennis?

No, not since father had trouble with his water. He has to go every half hour now. We hardly ever see him these days.

Otherwise engaged, I suppose. He must spend a hell of a lot of time in the toilet. Old age can be cruelty itself. Do you believe in God, Jim?

Occasionally. I'm not a regular at church though, never have been. I lean towards the Buddhists if I lean towards anything. I like the way they ring bells and shave their heads. We had one of them working in accounts last winter. He wore a summer jacket even in the coldest weather. I admired him.

And I admire you, Jim. Would you marry me? I'm sick to death of Fred, his pullovers with holes in, his constant writing to victims of contagious diseases, his insistence on chopping down trees in the back garden when I'm trying to sleep. I want to divorce.

So sudden, Lydia. I'll have to think about it. Are you pensionable? Are you prepared to massage mother's feet twice a day? There are dozens of things to be sorted out. Can you sleep with the light on?

If I have to…. Yes.

Wonderful. I hate searching for my slippers in the dark. Love, Lydia…has it arrived? I feel my whole body is about to break out into a rash. I'm itching like hell. Is that a good sign?

It's those shorts of yours, Jim. You leave yourself open to all kinds of infections. Winter's coming. It's time to wear something more substantial.

Whatever you say, Lydia.

That's right fatty. Ever thought about losing some weight as well?

JUNIOR

They say Junior cut the head off his pet tortoise before he ascended to heaven. Those that believe this kind of gossip are nothing more than jealous creeps. Junior was the best there was, a child with a heart the size of a great country mansion. I heard him recite the whole of King Lear before he was three years old. His mother, my sister Cindy, said he remembered it all after reading it through once. Cindy would never lie to me. Our father beat the hell out of us just in case we'd grow up bullshitters. We didn't.

Our neighbours are building a shrine to Junior out of seashells. I've lent them three candlesticks from my dead mother's private collection. I thought of giving them her mother of pearl rosary beads as well but changed my mind after their dog pissed on my doormat. Out of town people never control their pets properly.

Junior was almost six years old when he left this earth. His popularity with friends and neighbours was astounding. Last Christmas he received so many gifts we had to pass some of them to a local children's home. The little master took it very well. "The Lord provides for all," I remember him saying as he handed over an action man for parcelling up. His generous nature was legendary. None of us have ever forgotten the time he made a present of his laptop computer to a gypsy child at the cancer clinic he attended. He had a wisdom and compassion beyond his tender years. Why did the great man in the sky have to take him so young?

Cindy tells me that Billy Osprey, local psychic and new age nut, has been receiving messages from Junior regularly for weeks now. I'm sceptical. Billy's love for the bottle is well known. I've heard he talks to Winston Churchill when he's in his cups. Strong drink can do fearsome things to a bloke's imagination if it takes hold. I'd sooner remember Junior as he was when he was with us: golden haired, slightly pot bellied, singing "Yesterday" by the Beatles in a loud, tuneless voice. I'm sure he's walking hand in hand with the Lord at this very moment. My belief in the afterlife was drummed into me by my mother. She used to pull my ears hard if I didn't say my prayers at night.

Junior sometimes sat on the back porch in his little rocking chair talking to our feathered friends. I'll never forget a ferocious looking blackbird he befriended once. It was amazingly intelligent, could converse fluently in four languages. Junior said it had learnt to type out a letter as well, although I never saw it in action. That little chap's rapport with the natural world was something to behold. People came from streets away to have words with him. Cindy could have sold him to a travelling circus several times over. There were loads of offers.

"Life's a steaming cup of cappuccino," said Junior once after he'd been discussing Walt Whitman's verse with a visiting American professor. I recollect smiling to myself in the living room mirror when I heard him, shaking my head in wonderment at the simple, telling truth of his statement. Where did it all come from? Was it genetic? Cindy's ex-husband (and Junior's father) once trained to be a steeplejack, fell off at least three church roofs head first before he gave it up as a bad job. I'm informed he has visions now, is a wizard with rare equatorial plants, has written several books about humming birds. I haven't met him since he deserted Junior and Cindy at a Christmas party we were attending together in Waterloo Avenue. Could it be possible that the little one's brilliance came from him? I'm certain it wasn't from our side of the family. Mother and father were professional wrestlers. I have a suspicion they were both almost brain dead in their later years.

Junior ascended to heaven two days before my birthday. Three neighbours saw him leave. When pressed, one of them said, "He just jumped off the top of that little slide of his, flew straight upwards flapping his arms like a bird." Did the Lord call out to him, infuse him with a special strength? Cindy thinks so (she was in the bathroom drying her hair when it happened - couldn't hear him because of the noise she was making). She says all the lights in the house suddenly switched themselves on after he left, calming her somehow, ensuring that the shock of discovering his empty bed wasn't a shock at all.

I go to church every Sunday these days. Some of my friends don't approve. "You've lost your sense of humour," is the usual complaint or, "You're not the happy old drunk we used to know anymore." I couldn't care less. Our family has been touched by the spirit. How many of them

can claim to have a saint in the family? Cindy's thinking about writing to Pope John Paul in Rome. "I want to tell him about the time Junior brought his pet goldfish back from the dead," she said last time we talked on the telephone. "I'm sure I saw the fish smile after he'd done it."
Nothing surprises me about our late, great little angel. Each time I go to a record shop and look through the classical section I'm reminded of him. Junior could sing every part in every Verdi opera before he was four years old.

My ex-wife rang me up last week asking for an increase in child support. "You've got two daughters here you haven't spoken to for months," she yelled. "You're only interest is in that snobby dead nephew of yours. It's time you got a proper job, provided the necessary cash to look after your own. I'll never forget the time you funded that little swine's trip to Disneyland. Your precious sweeties here sobbed for days after they heard about it. Why didn't you pay for them?" I slammed the phone down. My family on the other side of town didn't exist as far as I'm concerned. The hurt caused after my girls called me "fatty face" and "smelly socks" in the shopping mall still causes pain. Junior was the child I always wanted. He never called me insulting names.

My last girl friend was a former nun, a beautiful girl who left the cloisters after a lesbian relationship with a red haired schoolteacher from Dublin. It was a turbulent sort of affair, ending with her attempted suicide in my bedroom one Saturday afternoon. I was never lucky in love. Even my childhood sweetheart had a sex change. Junior's short time on this planet of ours was a welcome light in my life. His knowledge of the continent of Africa still astounds me today. Some nights ago I had a dream about him dancing with a crowd of Zulus in heaven. Many of the men involved weren't wearing shorts or trousers. Junior didn't seem to mind though. Nakedness wasn't a thing that bothered him at all.

PARROT

I'm a parrot. He keeps talking to me, wanting me to repeat what he says. I won't do it. "Maureen's got a pair of legs like line props with woodworm," he's saying. "Fat Jimmy at number two cooks dead rats in olive oil." What does he think I am? Stupid? I was a happy as happy can be till they caught me in a net and shipped me down the Orinoco. It's purgatory plus here. If I had hands I'd suffocate him with one of those big fat embroidered cushions he plonks his backside on.
"Fierce Fiona sleeps with a frankfurter in her left ear. Colin eats nothing but fish fingers and shits in a bucket at the foot of the stairs." There he goes again. Why doesn't he go to the pub and woo that big bosomed barmaid he's always going on about? This torture's been going for over six months now. I'm close to jamming my head through the bars of my painfully small cage and strangling myself. I'm fifty-eight years of age this weekend. I need my peace.

What the hell's going on in the kitchen? Lord Nelson, his surprisingly good-natured pit bull terrier, sounds like he's smashing all the crockery up. I've never heard him bark so loud. Mind you, it's a bit of relief for me. He's finally stopped jabbering and gone to sort things out. Oh dear, what's that? He's screaming like a pig in a slaughterhouse. Has that pit bull taken a piece out of his leg? It sounds like he's in terrible pain. Ah, silence. I'll have a little talk out loud to myself to fill the void. Nothing he's tried to teach me though. Here I go: "The nights in Serbia can be cold and wet but the warmth of their women warms the cockles of the heart. A tyke on a tricycle can be torture to train well. Four Amazon crocodiles can eat a man in under ten minutes, especially one with a fat belly and soiled underwear." Oh, what's this? He's back and bleeding badly from the right leg. Are those tears in his eyes? He's ranting away like a lunatic. "I broke his neck with a single blow of the yard brush. He didn't so much as yelp. I had to teach him a lesson. That piece of steak on the draining board was for my supper, for my sole delight after a hard day's work. Our great guide up above will forgive me. If he doesn't he can go and thrust his head in a saucepan full of baked beans."
My goodness. What a fuss and bother.
That dog of his seems to have breathed his last. Shame. And all for snatching a bit of steak off the draining board! Rough justice I call it.

What if I accidentally shit in his cup of coffee one morning when I'm in the middle of my breakfast time gymnastics? Will he lose his temper, strangle the life out of me, squash me into the carpet with those great big feet of his? I'd rather be back up the Orinoco with fleas in my feathers. Life in this suburban dwelling is starting to become a trial. I wish his wife would come back from her holidays with her sister. She puts him in his place when he's out of order.

Great relief.
The last ten minutes have been pleasantly quiet. What is it about the evening paper that attracts my changeable owner so? He's totally absorbed in the second-hand ads again. Could it be he's searching for yet more junk to stuff into that overcrowded back room of his? Oh the times I've heard his wife complain about it. The arguments are horrendous. It wouldn't surprise me if she left him for good one of these days. He bought twenty pop-up toasters and a collection of false limbs a few weeks ago. She went bananas, tipped over the table with all the tea things on it. Her face turned bright red. I thought she was about to have a heart attack.

Ah, he's suddenly shot off into the kitchen. I can hear the rustle of paper. It sounds like he's wrapping Lord Nelson up ready for the dustmen. I wonder if he'll have to tip them to take the corpse away? City workers can be most choosy about what rubbish they take. I hope I get a proper burial in the garden when the big bird upstairs calls me in. The thought of my corpse being flung into a dustcart with a load of rotting vegetables makes my whole body shiver. What a surprise! He's back in the living room already, and talking to himself again. I sense a mental breakdown coming on. His voice is unusually high.
"Where did Madge put the mincing machine? I can't let all that dog flesh go to waste. Burgers and chips, lots of burgers and chips. We can put it all in the deep freezer. It'll take months to polish off. Our bill at the butcher's will be down to zero. We'll be able to visit Eric in Malta with the money saved. I've been wanting to walk the streets of Valetta for years now. I wonder if Eric's still got the chest expander I sent him last Christmas?"
I'm uneasy. He's moving closer to my cage, waving his arms about wildly. I'll pretend to be asleep.
"You stupid parrot. Why can't you talk like the last resident of that rusty old cage of yours? He could recite the whole menu from Mario's restau-

rant at the drop of a hat. If there was a parrot university he would have won a first class degree."

What a coarse and ill-mannered chap he is.

A parrot with my exotic forebears (one of them spent twenty happy years in Berlin zoo) shouldn't have to put up with his kind of behaviour. Thank God he's decided to go back into the kitchen. I thought my days as a household pet were numbered.

What shall I do now?

Sing, shit, make gurgling noises in my water pot? No. I'll practice my human voice again, test my vocabulary a little. Here goes:
"Anthea's got ants in her knickers, boils cabbage in her mother's old boots, keeps a bucket of beetroot under the bed. Uncle Ned's war medals are somewhere at the bottom of the Atlantic Ocean. Derek's mother lost his khaki Boy Scout trousers in the cinema last week. A boiled ostrich egg with buttered toast is the perfect start to a busy working day. Men over forty-five should never wear trainers in public."

I'd better stop. He's here again, and carrying a bloodstained carving knife. What the hell has he been up to now? My beak suddenly feels cold. It's always a sign of nervousness. He's muttering away at great speed. I can hardly tell what he's saying.

"What did she do with that mincing machine? Cutting old Nelson up by hand is damned hard work. I mustn't give in though. I'll hack him into manageable pieces now and buy a new mincer tomorrow. Nothing ventured nothing gained. The enormous saving in burger meat will make it all worthwhile. I'll tell Madge the dog was run over by a bus."

He's looking for something in the sideboard drawer. The early evening summer light's casting dark shadows on his bony face. Now he's staring at me again, knife poised in a threatening position. "I'll get you to talk if it's the last thing I do. Say Madge's big sister has a nose like a rotten carrot. Madge's father slept with old tarts during the war. I like a fat cucumber up my arse. Speak! Speak! Speak!"

I'm doing my best, but I seem to have lost my voice. From a jungle over the ocean to a psychopath's semi-detached in Nottingham. He's taken off one of his slippers and he's about to throw it. I hope it doesn't hit my cage and knock all the water out of my pot. I'm the thirstiest parrot I know. I could die of dehydration before his wife gets back. He hasn't cleaned out my cage once since she's been away.

PSYCHOSIS IN THE SUNSHINE:
MY SUMMER HOLIDAY, 1995

If I am to die please allow me time to laugh. Give me jolly brainstorms, wide-reaching spasms to curl the toes. Send tingles up and down this fractured, blistered frame. I'm golden. I dream speak. I'm already in a sort of heaven.

It was raining today and I thought of you. "If you're truly psychic you can reach me," you said shortly before our parting. I tried this afternoon. The fleas and moths spoiled my reverie. This current hot spell has played havoc with the concentration.

"It's the year of the pig," said a paunchy drunk in the plane coming over here. "We're all slipping into the pit. Obnoxious behaviour is about to become the norm." I pressed the buzzer for a stewardess. "I want to change my seat!" I shouted. "This man's trying to shit on me spiritually." A slanging match developed. "Cunt," he shrieked. "Powderpuff of the cosmos," I bellowed. Then it turned into fisticuffs; hair pulling, shirt ripping. Eventually, the stewardess silenced us both with well-chosen karate blows. Women of the sky are formidable. I have a bruised neck to prove it.

I don't want to die in a boarding house. Imagine passing slowly away in a building inhabited by guests buttering toast and pouring tea in the breakfast room. It would be necessary for Jesus Christ to appear before me to explain the situation. My faith would need shoring up.

Why am I golden? What evidence is there for me to make such an outlandish claim? I suggest it's the light. There's no one here to measure its density, appreciate (with their imagination) its intensity. I'm frequently alone. My truthfulness has to be taken on trust.

Three nights ago I had a nightmare about a beach hut catching fire. "There's a child inside," wailed somebody from the crowd. Middle aged family men wearing baggy shorts filled buckets with water from the sea, rushed with purpose to douse the flames. When the child emerged he was as black as the devil. "Bloody lucky to be alive," commented a rescuer. I found myself wondering if he'd survive.

The sight of his cracked and crooked little arms caused me to have huge doubts.

Then there was the hotel in Bali, five Germans in the next room. I didn't like them. "Tolerance," you said, as we tried to sleep through their loud music. "We were young once." But I wouldn't have it. I complained and got socked on the jaw for my pains. You didn't even bother to pick me up. "Bastards of your ilk deserved to grovel in the dirt," you snarled, a high heeled shoe poised dangerously close to my left ear.

Why does death fascinate me so? I'm on holiday. I slouch carelessly in a canvas beach chair. I wish to become a carefree zombie.
"And can you hear the ghostly steamships entering the harbour?" a person inquires, squeezing my hand with a frightening animal ferocity. "No," I reply feeling for my icy heart and finding nothing.

You're here somewhere. I expect a visitation before the holiday is over. Maybe we'll cross paths on the beach? Whisper to me through the kitchen window before I go to bed - please tell me what you'll be wearing. Something fancy I hope. A chicken head with feathers sticking out of the hole in your arse. You laughed out loud at me last time we met. I'd like my revenge.

When we depart we instantly come back again. All relationships are renewed, slanderous comments erased. Here and now is a half way house, a sort of heaven for nutcases and normals alike.
It is written: "Take upon yourself the responsibility for your own imagination." Whoever wrote this (and I suspect it was me) had more than a whiff of crap up his nostrils at the time. Socks stink, fat drunks make puddles in the corner of our bedroom. I'm losing all. I could lose my underpants to a stranger.

2

Today finds me effortlessly effusive. Holidays (especially this one) bring out the potential jollity in me. I love the doughnut people here, their philandering bottom pinching ways. The disco is alive with their presence. I salute the man who operates the laser show, his ability to illuminate the holes in their heads.

Will I need a wheelchair soon? Will it be necessary to push me up and down the promenade to make me crack a smile? My legs buckle in readiness. The hotel breakfast room spins round. A sweet signora (as round as a baby in a Rubens) asks if I'm O.K.
We visit a well-known waterfall tomorrow. I've asked for a limousine to take us there. Craig, our driver for the day, will more than likely try to break my wrists at the traffic lights. When servants become masters some harmless soul always gets his. It was like this in Bali. My beautiful baby face encourages nasty behaviour.

There's to be no more buttock baring for giggles.
I'm giving it up. I've also placed a personal ban on red plastic noses, zebra striped codpieces, lurid green wigs speckled silver. I'm nobody's fool now. I wish to vacation with dignity. The days when I'd liven up a holiday by bursting into hotel lounge shouting, "I'm a greasy fat sausage and everybody here's a dozy dickhead," are numbered. My physical decline has played a big part in this decision. The sad sag in my rear end has turned me wary.

Today could be a day for sucking on a seagull's beak, closing the end up with my steely lips. They're noisy. They nibble holes into sneakers. I despise the confidence that this sea, sand and bracing air gives them. If we are to be owners of the universe we must stop their insolence. Who gave them the right to perch on pushchairs and frighten sunburnt babies? Who gave them permission to huddle on windowsills and watch us enviously through the dining room window?
Respect is called for. Holidaymakers everywhere must assert themselves.

You're messing up my mind again. I hate it. Doesn't my deep felt need for a truce impress you at all? Lord knows, I'm the blandest of bland creatures these days. When I enter a room I disappear. I'm now the nobody you always wanted me to be. Isn't it enough?

We're going home soon. Craig's driving us to the airport, washing the car in the courtyard as I write. I'd like to ask him (but I'm just a tiny bit afraid) if his mother received the flowers I sent her. He's a wonderful son to the old bitch. I feel sure he'll appreciate the gesture when he gets to know about it.

"Suicide would be too easy a way out," you yelled once when I was teetering, sobbing on a Cornish cliff top. Slow torture would be better. I seem to recall a passing stranger reprimanding you for your callousness. "Give the poor cunt a chance," was all he said. My, you were so angry! I thought you'd never let go of his balls. It was a relief when the police dogs came. The sight of them tearing at your jeans with their big yellow teeth induced a glow of security that remained in my body for days afterwards.

I believe in mermaids, barbarian fishtailed maidens with love in their eyes. After midnight I hear them sporting in the cove, skidding lightly across waves. When I mention my sightings to the residents in the T.V. lounge they advise me to see a doctor. I pity them. To be born without the sensitivity to see and hear God's most exotic creatures is a potentially crippling problem, I would like to help them but I can't. Their scorn has turned me numb.

3

I think I see the future and it's marvellous out there. Jeremy Lightbody, my guide in most of these matters, is bullish about it all. "Go ahead and believe," he says from his favourite position beneath the bedside lamp, "flood your system with it." Tonight I'm a tall tree in a steaming hot jungle with rowdy parrots on my branches. I hear the hyena and I'm not afraid. The mundane is for monkeys. I eat their eyes out.

"Nothing can stop the sea," you said, seven days before our parting. I lashed out at you with a tea towel. I'm sorry now. The freshness of your vision should have astounded me. My grey growling machismo spoilt everything. Oh silent sea, insist eternity is kind to me.

I knew the toast would be burnt at breakfast and that a fat fly would succeed in trapping himself in the marmalade. Visions made of trivia overtake me sometimes. Being psychic isn't all angels and heavenly choirs. I once told Craig his future was in opening a garage near Marble Arch. His response was to kick my shins. There are many amongst us who don't appreciate my gift.

Soon we'll be on the road. I shall be sad (naturally) but more than a little optimistic. Look out when I pass the golden galleon in the harbour as I'll probably yell "Hooray" and squeeze my naked bottom out of the car window to promote a laugh. I will be as I've always been. My lack of fear is my greatest asset. Tonight I'll rummage through drawers, savage your house pets, pee copiously into those mamby pamby cribs you put your kiddies in.

When the devil in me moves, I'm a fiend. Can you hear the sea boiling? Time to make the tea. Time to charm the snakes out of the knots in my hair.

TACITURN TOMKINS

This bleak land (mountains like boozers' noses, the stink of rotting fish wafting from the bushes) is so bad it kills the thought of any erection. I'm stifled when I look at it. I need the sea, scorpions in the bedclothes to chew at my toenails; cancer.
Shouting, "Allah be praised," in a synagogue makes heavenly sense to me. Now I'm out of their hospital I can do any bloody thing I like.
But you might ask, as you're perfectly entitled to do. "Does she love you as much as she did before you went nuts?" It's a question that has no need for an answer. Look at my socks! Aren't they the living end in tidy darning?

So I'm in the garden (brash the birdsong, ominous the steeple beyond the topiary) cleaning up my act.
Cheesy, my faithful Jack Russell, toys with a bone the size of the erection I wished I could achieve, and laughs.
"Gulah Gulah" he goes (mocking in tone – silly really) and I'm made to know he knows more than I could ever know. Shamed, I slump to the lawn with fists afire. I resolve to punch a hole in my neighbour's nasty plaited fence – later.

And then (dark the morning, fierce the rain on the kitchen window) an argument over breakfast. Feisty I am, all popping eyes and pinging pyjama jacket buttons. Taciturn Tompkins is what they should call me. She starts it but I finish it. Throwing eggs about frightens her.

I'm resigned to my nature; cherish it in fact. At least I'm not some arse-licking stick-in-the-mud pisspot with a job that bores him to death. I'm O.K. "Bill wants you," says my nympho friend from the hospital. Who am I to disagree with this importuning imp of a precious creature, this warm and willing sylph of lust? Sacred be the body that God gave her.

Must I work? The idle life suits me. I think it would be better if I didn't. Work disturbs my little illnesses, eradicates their teasingly cruel divine influence on my well-being; makes me well in fact. I don't want to concentrate on any task. I want to sleep and flounder, flip flop blind through the days. My bottom lip drops as I think, this giving me the appearance of fish begging for the hook. If you were watching now you would probably be amused.

Only she could send me back there. I heard her talking on the phone this morning using words like "idle" and "demented," "fables" and "fanciful." The bitterness in her voice made me cringe. She had to be talking about me. The doctors believe her every word.

Then there's Jesus. His eyes are everywhere. He's at the back of every meaningful stare. During my last spell in that hospital I thought I saw him talking to an old lady at the bus stop. When I told the chaplain he had me transferred to occupational therapy. "It'll keep you out of harms way," he said. It didn't. I half strangled fat Harry Burdett over a game of dominoes a couple of weeks later.

I could have been considerably more than I've turned out to be. It's my proneness to all forms of delirium that's been the bind. I'm a marked man. She wasn't the right choice for me. I was pushed into it. If only they'd taught us more about sex at school. Catastrophe after catastrophe has frayed me at the edges, turned this potentially useful member of society into a layabout.

When I find the strength I'll rip up his prize roses and smash every pane of glass in his greenhouse. Why should I take his insults? What right has he got to leave his excrement on my doorstep next to her lovely clean milk bottles? He thinks I'm not fit to sit in my own back garden (he said as much through the wall last night); seems to want to introduce malice and fear into my every waking moment. I'm not about to buckle. She knows how strong willed I can be. Wasn't it me who did the shoplifting for her when she fell ill?

Rats are fatter than cats in parts of Iraq and sleep (this is information I've gathered recently) is frightfully hard to come by in some African states. Imagine the penury and pain some of us have to go through in order to gesticulate freely. Democracy is rooted in free access to all our limbs. Madness is a sword.

When I've removed her head I shall present it to the city fathers as evidence. "This," I'll roar, "is what turned the corner for me." Then they'll stutter and flutter and cough like cancerous crabs, their arms squiggling in all fucking directions. Then bow-ties will spin; watches will stop. I'll see to it.

I've heard the madhouses in Cairo are stuffed with bald headed idiots shouting "Mercy Allah" and banging their heads against walls. It's not like that here. Our places of refuge are homely. I had my own washbasin and toilet last time I was in. Nurse Bray (he was in charge of all we did and said) was a model of compassion and fair play; a saint in starchy white. He never tweaked my ears once.

When people laugh at me I'm inclined to throw them down. My temper has often been my undoing. Craig Brown felt the brunt of it once when I caught him making faces behind my back at summer camp. I was the angriest cub in our pack. Three of the scouts couldn't hold me back. I punched and punched and punched till his nose nearly fell off. Even our club master licked my arse out of fear afterwards.

After I've severed her limbs from her torso I'll bury them under the apple tree. It'll have to be deep though. I can't have Cheesy digging her up again. A Jack Russell is a tenacious beast, without peer in the realms of dogdom; curious to a fault and cheeky beyond a joke.
Who made him so?
God? Jack Russell?

I have a secret. John Atkins, former drinking partner and a candidate for the priesthood, lies buried in my cellar. I was between jobs when I did it. He shouldn't have insulted me. Nobody likes being called a simpleton, especially when they're drunk. My hitting him over the head with a heavy glass ashtray seemed like a reasonable response to unreasonable provocation at the time. I'm not so sure now.

Whilst staring intensely at myself in the mirror the other day I discovered a small brown wart above my left eyebrow. "Cancer," I screamed, calling for her to make an inspection. "Cancer! Cancer! Cancer!" she raced in to the bathroom immediately.

"Let me look," she said sweetly, rapidly. "I'm sure it's nothing to worry about." I felt better immediately. It's marvellous what a frightened slave of a woman can do for one's peace of mind.

The hospital is almost my second home. In recent years I've come to know every shrub and bush on the main driveway, almost every wilting flowerbed. Quite a few of the staff have become personal friends. I've always liked nurses bearing strong tranquillizers. Sleep will be difficult tonight. I can hear cats already, sense the angst in the rats they're about to pursue. It could be time to throw all the windows open and let the moths and fleas in, let them fluster the bad vibrations with their busy little row. I'm touched by every damn thing that happens in the world. My body is a planet before its time.

She doesn't sleep with me now. I gave her permission. "Not necessary," I recall saying as she pretended to be upset by my decision. "I know my night-time oratory keeps you awake." She still changes my sheets though. Dirty bed linen encourages rodents.

Tomorrow is the big day. Nobody kicks Cheesy up the arse and gets away with it. She's got to go. I'll do it in the kitchen.

Then there's his nibs, my know-it-all neighbour with the staring eyes. He'll get his at the weekend. I'll do it in the dark when he's crawling back from the pub. Two karate chops to the neck and he's kaput. Easy stuff.

I crave peace, squirm in my bed with delight when I think about it. What's wrong with wanting a house with all the curtains drawn and the television switched off? My needs are simple. My heart pounds at the thought of finally reaching my goal.

TOPSY TURVY TIME

The hillbilly screams, torn trousers tumble, somebody eats a fried sausage on a stick noisily. Then cats prowl, talking like kiddies to themselves, annoying us all. Then Mr. Nobody sits outside the mall with a cardboard box on his head pretending to be some kind of emperor. Police carrying a large assortment of lethal weapons arrest him. It's pay back time.

Charlene

Yes Mr. Pumpkin

Call out the dogs, load up the ice cream buckets, make play with fried chicken sandwiches. Life is a selection of unnecessary events turned important by excessive use of whipping cream and Hershey bars, a bedazzling feast of lemon meringue pie served in a glistening diner to overweight school chums. If there's to be a change we must trap the mice in the bathroom.

But Mr. Pumpkin, is it necessary to make such a fuss about it all? Your fancy words are simply an attempt to make the tedious fascinating. The mice in the bathroom have made their home there and they like it. Why crush their necks when all they do is scrounge a little electricity, nibble at old bars of soap and forgotten pieces of toast? I was taught to radiate goodness at Sunday school. Let all creatures live as they wish to live. Tolerance Mr. Pumpkin, tolerance.

Charlene dissolves in a large bowl of deep brown gravy. Somebody sings a popular country and western classic as they boil peas to a sticky green mush. Mr. Pumpkin lights the candle inside his head, strides out into the clammy West Virginia night. A chorus of bats squeak love songs on the roof of the Christian Science community centre. Everything is somehow as it should be. Reason, in all its magnificent unreasonableness, seems to prevail.
Voices can be heard at the end of the street...

And you Martha Greenhorn, would you cut out the heart on an innocent baby if asked?

What a question Mathew Froginall. We Americans are a God-fearing bunch. The teachings of Jesus Christ forbid such voodoo trickery. Because my skin is black doesn't mean I'm a monster. Saintly Martha they call me. I have my seat reserved in the Baptist chapel. Preachers and trainee missionaries court me on a regular basis. I fuck and fuck and fuck some weekends.

Such strident language Miss Martha, such vulgar boldness. You really were close to being a saint when we were at high school. What happened to the sweetie we all knew? I suspect you have a hole in your soul, a chink in your spiritual armour. Are you stable mentally?

No. I was in the State madhouse for a long spell. I got caught eating a live bullfrog. The Lord told me to do it and I did it. I ate it with French fries.

You're lying. You're lying to please me because you know I'm a lawyer and rich. Could it be you're expecting a small financial reward of some kind? God doesn't approve of this kind of behaviour. I thought you were a regular chapelgoer. He that has the power will punish you if you continue in this fashion.

Fuck off you white assed, skinny, bullshitting pig. The Lord gave me the power to be what I want to be. I'm almost a saint. Who are you to say that I'm not? Have you had a word in the Lord's ear or something? You seem mighty sure of yourself.

Miss Martha, I'm one of God's helpers, one of the folks who organises justice for him when he's been wronged, one of the folks who washes his cup when he's had some coffee. I often boil his egg at breakfast. He's as close to me as my dear departed wife was.

Fatty Frognall, you're a prize turd face, a disgrace to the state of West Virginia. My father was a hard working man and never told a lie in his life. What's wrong with you? It seems to me you could do with a stay in that madhouse up the road.

Martha is suddenly buried under a collapsing pile of giant pancakes. Matthew Greenhorn ignores her screams, pours hot syrup all over them, squealing with pleasure as he does it.

A fire engine passes with sirens blazing away. Martha's book of food stamps lies in a pool of syrup on the sidewalk. Enter a giant holding a basketball, a packet of condoms plainly visible in his back pocket. Queen Sabrina's just returning from the Laundromat. She leaves a trail of damp stockings and lingerie as she makes her weary way home. Life's as tough as tough in Crack City.

Sabrina.

Yeah baby.

Ready to light my fire with a few of them hugs and kisses of yours, ready to get hot all over me? I'm the big guy you love to play ball with. I'm an old-fashioned lover man with attitude. I crush the whitey white with all my might, make soup with his bones. I'm a lot of things you don't even know about. Ready to give me a try?

Not yet baby. You got to clean up your act a little before I'll even think about it. What's all this racist shit you're coming out with? I love Mr. Whitey White. He kisses my ass most tenderly when I tell him to. I get him bending, bowing and almost scraping the damn sidewalk with his chin. He's servility personified in my company. Got my meaning big boy? I got no complaints about nothing from him. But it's hard here. I'm thinking of giving that crack stuff a try. What's it like?

Hold on baby. What's got into you? I'm a keep fit type of guy. I got muscles where they shouldn't even exist. I chop trees down in the woods for kicks. What would I want with drugs? Life's my drug. I love looking at my ass in the mirror.
Wise up honey.
Get yourself a piece of me and start to live again.

I'm ready.

A pause.

The author considers saying more about the people he's writing about, giving details of their age, state of teeth and taste in clothes. Unfortunately, his desire to aid the reader in this way falls foul of his natural laziness.
"They'll have to make the pictures up themselves," he grumbles, as he paces round his small flat.
"If they don't have enough imagination it's their own fault." A kettle starts to whistle in the kitchen. A small fat cat cowers under the writing desk, very wary of harsh, piercing noises.

The action continues. Sabrina shakes her head, trudges on up the road with her washing. The baseball giant, more than a little pissed at her rejection of him, throws his ball hard at a passing mongrel. A police car pulls up beside him. A white officer wearing big black sunglasses sticks his head of the window.

Why did you do that son? Don't you like dogs?

None of your business.

Oh yes it is. Folks like you just can't run around throwing heavy balls at dumb animals. You would have killed him if you'd hit him. Look at the size of you! You don't know your own strength.

Oh yes I do. I could strangle you with one hand behind my back if I had a mind to. I've been a potential killer from a very early age. Go and take a running jump. You guys make me sick. Haven't you got some real police work to do?

Like what?

Like saving old ladies from burning buildings, planting drugs on unsuspecting teenagers. There are a million and one things you should be doing. Go to it guy.

Officer, to you!

So sensitive.

Why not? My mother kept a flower shop in Pittsburgh and taught me to boil an egg before I could walk. I've got a gentle, domestic side to me. I always help with the ironing.

I'm not impressed. A cop is a cop to me. How do I know you're not going to shoot me in the back if I decide to run off? A stack of freshly pressed boxer shorts doesn't mean you're not a psychopath. I've heard Hitler liked to do a little dusting now and then.

Enough of the wisecracks. Wow, what's that?

A small flying saucer lands in front of the police car. A naked dwarf with big ears and a flashing light bulb attached to the top of his head emerges sulking from the machine. The baseball giant gathers his ball from the gutter, makes a quick dash for it. The officer sits open mouthed in his vehicle, transfixed. The dwarf speaks.

Coffee?

What?

Coffee. I want to drink a cup of that stuff I've heard so much about. Have you the water for boiling in that box on wheels you're sitting in? We've observed this unusual coffee habit of humans for years from afar. What is in the beans that make it so popular? Can a being like me, tired and weary after a long journey from the outer hemisphere, gain a little pleasure from it? Are you dumb or something? Answer!

Hey big ears, don't shout at me. I've the power to arrest you for obstructing traffic and walking around in the nude. Who are you anyway? One of those sick students from upstate? I haven't seen a weirdo like you since Woodstock. What's with the light bulb on the head?

It helps clear my thoughts on gloomy Monday mornings, adds a flicker of light to the proceedings when I'm cycling through the dark craters at home. We are practical, peace loving creatures. Why do you carry a weapon?

To kill sneaky little bastards like you, lie face down on the sidewalk, spread your legs! You're a suspicious character just about to get himself in big trouble. All this crap about coffee. I think you're a communist on a mission.

O.K. I'll do what you say. It seems pretty pointless though. All you're going to see is the hole in my arse. Ah well, this planet of yours isn't as friendly as some of my colleagues led me to believe. It seems to me some of them have been tuning in to too many of those eternal sunshine and happy natives type of T.V. holiday programmes. I'll give them hell when I get back.

Get down big ears, now!

O.K., O.K., O.K. leave that dangerous weapon of yours in its holster. I know when an interplanetary fool like myself has drawn the short straw. Relax.

As if by magic, and magic it possibly is, a big choir of blond haired Norwegian boys surround the police officer. Their leader, a large hairy youth wearing a cassock and brandishing an oversized wooden crucifix, kicks the startled cop up the backside.

Take that you American bullyboy! We have God and a million ice maidens on our side. Compassion begins with a clean toilet seat. Have you wiped that fat arse of yours today?
The cop blushes, puts his gun back in its holster, pulls at his belt buckle nervously.

Want to see?

The traveller from outer space returns to his small spacecraft and with ears flapping rapidly enters the main door, fires up the engine, leaves. The Norwegian choir applauds loudly. Their burly leader is particularly enthusiastic.

What wonders those little persons up there have accomplished. Don't you find it remarkable that people with such large ears have been able to achieve so much? Mankind hasn't got the brain for it. The best he can do is equip idiots like you with dangerous weapons officer, teach them how to kill. We Norwegians don't like what we see in America. I haven't been able to make a decent snowball in weeks.

Snow!

Yes Mr. Policeman, snow! That white stuff that flutters from the sky in Hollywood films. Don't you have it here? Is it always as hot as this?

This is the land of fleas. My wife was bitten all over the ear lobe last night. Her itching and scratching kept me awake till four this morning. I almost smothered her to death with a pillow. In my job a good night's rest is very necessary. I get hot flushes if I don't sleep properly.

Oh dear, hot flushes mean psychopathic tendencies where I come from. Have you ever tried reindeer meat with scrambled eggs? It soothes the soul, turns a madman into an angel. King Haakon had it for breakfast the day before he died. I hear he giggled with pure pleasure for ten minutes after he'd finished. It was the talk of Oslo.

Hacking…who the fuck is King Hacking?
Are you trying to deliberately make a fool on an officer of the law? I should arrest you and your crowd for blocking up the sidewalk. Where did you guys come from anyway? Sometimes I think I'm losing my brain cells. Why does the good Lord keep springing surprises on me?

Another pause.

The author, ever mindful of the fictional monster he's creating, finds himself sitting on the toilet thinking of a suitable finish to it all. "I've got to move the action to somewhere else," he says, reaching for a piece of toilet paper to blow his nose on, "England in summer perhaps." A small group of big-eared Martians gather at the washbowl, start fiddling with the taps. "How primitive and pointless," mutters their leader, trying not no be heard. He has awful memories of humans and their aggressive ways. Everyone on the planet's heard about the time he had to show the hole in his arse to a West Virginia cop. The author, however, is oblivious to everything. His late evening shit is a vital part of his normal day. Complete concentration is very necessary.

End of pause. The scene moves to an English country garden in the middle of June. Three sun tanned, middle class ladies are taking afternoon tea. The one with dyed blonde hair and wearing pink shorts speaks first.

Our eldest boy's a devil of a trial at the moment, quite beyond the pale. This morning at breakfast he kept talking about three alcoholic Martians who'd visited him in the middle of the night, said they'd given him a bottle of elderberry wine and some cheese snacks. Sometimes I wonder if he's on crack or something. It's a terrific worry. He's only thirteen.

The youngest of the trio, overweight thirty-two year old with two difficult daughters sympathises….

Oh dear. Aren't kids a trial? My little one ate four cheeseburgers at one sitting in the city yesterday. I don't know where she gets her money from. I've a strong feeling she steals from her father's piggy bank. I wouldn't have got to know about it if her sister hadn't snitched on her. There was a terrific wrestling match on the lounge carpet afterwards.

The third member of the group remains silent. She's childless and heading for a divorce because of it. All talk about youngsters makes her sad.

Suddenly there's a ferocious snorting in the bushes and an extremely fat pig wearing a spotted bathing suit and walking on his hind legs emerges. His manner exudes extreme self-confidence. He's the king of all pigs as far as he's concerned, the smartest old hog this universe of ours has ever seen. With a grunt and a gurgle he struts up to the lady wearing pink shorts, addresses her in his best high class English.

How are you my little sweetmeat? I see you're wearing those chic pink shorts again. Nice colour. My kind of hue. Your bottom looks a treat in them. What does that husband of yours think? Does he get jealous when men stare at you?

The woman appears to know the pig and, much to the surprise of her companions, reaches out to shake his left trotter. There's great affection in her voice when she talks to him.

Hello Porky, still hiding in the bushes I see, still spying on humans in that nosy, sneaky way of yours. Isn't it time you surrendered to the butcher and turned yourself into some nice streaky bacon slices? Sorry. Didn't mean it. Just joking. How's that overfed young wife of yours? Still giving you problems?

Not at the moment Mrs. Wimple, not at the moment. Our last three months together have been marital bliss. That little wooden hut we share together has never been so clean and tidy. And she's learnt to cook Mrs. Wimple! Last night she made the biggest and best cheese and onion pie I've ever tasted. The crust was a dream, so crunchy....

The overweight thirty-two year old, amazed and confused to the point of hysteria, interjects loudly.

Pies! What do you know about pies? I've been making the best pastry in England for the past five years. My mother, the serial killer Bertha Hardwick, taught me all she knew before they put her away. I remember her thrashing me with a leather belt in the kitchen when one of my apple pies didn't rise properly.

Did she pull your pants down?

The blonde with the pink shorts is suddenly bright eyed and alert. Her companion's talking about something she has deep interest in. Bottom spanking is one of her more perverse pastimes. Her children, husband and the silent member of the group who is about to get divorced are willing participants in her "games." She's known as "Glenda the buttock basher" to friends and foes alike. The sight of raw, red backside has been known to make her sob with joy. There's a giggle in her voice as she questions her friend further.

How many times did your mother strike you? Did she make you lie across a stool? Oh I wish I could have been there. I love kitchen-spanking sessions. Where you wearing a pinafore at the time?

The pig retreats into the bushes.

See you folks. I've got to get back home and do a spot of gardening. Can I borrow your watering can Mrs. Wimple? My rose bushes must be dying of thirst.

And so finishes the English part of this rambling little talk. The author wipes his arse, adjusts his clothing and returns to his "thinking chair" by the spluttering solitary radiator. "It's topsy turvy time," he says out loud. "Nothing seems to fit. It's all that time travelling, fancy computers and the like, I want us all to lie flat in a field full of buttercups, stare up the blue, blue sky. People mix each other up. We should all shut our mouths and say nothing. Silence is divine. Blabber and blither make me puke."

The author pauses to fart four times. Switch to a small bar in Oslo. A jolly group of Norwegian youths are gathered round a log fire farting in harmony. A buxom, middle-aged woman in a long velvet evening dress is conducting them with great panache. The loudest of the young farters starts a conversation with her. She speaks in a shrill voice that sounds something akin to a schizophrenic parrot on heat.

Well Mrs. Gluwein, what do you think?

It smells Michael, but it's good.

Nice to know it. Nice to know we are farting together in the correct way. I've thought of bringing a small combo into this building next week to play along with us. Would you agree with that? Could you direct operations in the normal way? Leopold Stokowski was very difficult in new situations. How would you be?

Perfectly alright young man. My hot temper would be under a tin lid all night. My late husband said I was a fireball. We would shout at each other in rooms. How is it at home for you?

Perfectly alright, although my extra hard farting upsets my grandfather. He's threatened suicide lots of times in the past year. Mother laughs about it, has put a noose by his bed for a joke. The poor bastard is extremely old. Have you any opinions about homes for the senile and hard of hearing?

The farting is reaching a deafening climax. Mrs. Gluwein shouts to be heard above the row.

I have no wish to talk about it. Death is already a shadow across my naked thighs at night. I'm concerned about what to wear in heaven. Will a nightgown and strong underwear be enough?

A fierce explosion rocks the building and all within it are transported to America. As they fly through the air they fart, sing and play silly games with each other. Mrs. Gluwein has a fireball under her evening gown, travels much faster than the others. Fate has purpose for her across the ocean but she's not sure what it is.

Now we're in West Virginia again, our intrepid police officer is lying in bed staring at the ceiling, his brain more than a little fogged up after a heavy night drinking with some members of the Norwegian choir. "Phew," he says, reaching for his socks, "phew, wow, oh!" A large red and yellow parrot on a perch in the house next door can be heard talking to itself through the paper-thin walls. "Castigate the rich," it says. "All power to those who live in squalor. We of the soil are the true inheritors of God's kingdom." The cop leaps out of bed and rushes to the window, naked.
"Today is the day of days," he shouts, flinging back the curtains and exposing himself to the world. "Today is the day King Hacking of Norway's ex girlfriend arrives to play tennis with me." "Hallelujah," calls the parrot through the walls. "Cover yourself up," yells a matronly passer-by with hair the colour of a forest fire. Then Mrs. Gluwein lands on the front lawn. Her long affair with our policeman starts from this point. His naked hairiness attracts her attention. A feverish conversation commences...

Oh Mr. Naked man, what a sight for sore eyes you are. I've been travelling at great speed in that big blue sky up there: almost thought I was going to pass out with the stress of it all. I'm not a rocket ship, not a firework to be blasted and blown about. The presence of a stationary human being on God's firm earth settles my churning stomach. How good it is to know that men with dangling things still let them dangle. How marvellous to discover that all humanity doesn't have to perpetually whiz about. I'm grateful to you Mr. Naked man, whoever you are.

Not a problem my dear. I'll just open this window a fraction more so I don't have to shout. It seems to me you've had quite a rough ride. When I get dressed you'll notice I'm an officer of the law, a tough, burglar-hating son of a gun. Excuse me while I slip into the other room and fetch my trousers. I don't want to offend you more than I have done already. A lady dressed as fine as you shouldn't need to put up with nudity. I can see you're a person with standards. What does your husband do? Does he hold a position in industry?

No, he's dead. When he was alive he travelled round Norway selling fish pies.

Ah, interesting. Did you know King Hacking?
I had a dream two nights ago, which featured Norway, snowballs, King Hacking and a woman with red lips like yours. A voice in the dream said I'd meet the woman and make love to her. Is it you? Where you Hacking's girlfriend?

King Haakon! My former lover man was the noble King Haakon. We used to meet by the sea and eat fish pies. He loved my husband's produce. We would fart a lot afterwards, terrifically smelly. If I mention this does it offend you? I don't mean it. Sometimes I say what comes directly into my brain. We people from the North are like this. Some people say I have a voice like a schizophrenic parrot on heat. Would you agree?

Schizo what? I don't know the word. All I know is I feel we've met before, that we've wined and dined and danced on another planet in another time, that you've made scrambled eggs for me at least four times in a past life. I love that long gown you're wearing. Do you realise there's a hole in the backside and I can see your pale blue underwear? Do you mind?

No. I've nothing to be ashamed of. What you see is what you're getting. Alright? Great. I'll go and open the back door so that you can come and join me for coffee. It's a little chilly this morning. You could catch your death of cold standing out on the front lawn with that hole in your dress.

We Norwegians know the coldness.
It isn't troubling me at all. By the way, you don't have to put your trousers on if you don't want to. I like your bareness, your dingly dongly private parts.

The author claps his hands. A Martian in a boiler suit and crash helmet arrives with a pot of tea and two cups on a tray. The alien looks nervous, his big ears itch like the very devil inside his helmet. When he speaks his nose turns purple.

You fell asleep in your chair. You were mumbling on about a Norwegian woman called Gluwein. Who is she? An old girlfriend? You earthlings are passionate sorts. What's this kissing about, and why do you want to smack Mrs. Gluwein's round bottom? Here's your tea. I heard you order it telepathically.

Oh, oh thanks, thanks. You must be one of those Martians I've been writing about. Have I got it right about the flying saucers? Do you really ride round the heavens in them? And what about the police in West Virginia? Is it usual for you to let them look up your arse?

I don't want to talk about such things. I'm the talk of Mars because of it. What about your fixation with farting racist baseball players, West Virginia, naughty Martha Greenhorn and the rest? I detect a diseased mind at work.

Really. How come?

Well, on Mars we think about sensible things. Life can be a puzzle without a solution. We're far too busy perfecting the design of our spacecraft to be amused by farters and their doings. We never laugh unless it's really necessary.

The author tires of the conversation, claps his hands, makes the Martian disappear. Then Queen Sabrina crosses his field of vision again. He goes to his desk, picks up a pen and pad, starts to write. He almost forgot she ever existed. He's glad she's back. Sabrina's eating breakfast in a little wooden house on the outskirts of Charleston, West Virginia. She's left the losers in Crack City and now works in a fancy diner just off the main highway. Her companion at the breakfast table, a balding fifty year old black man with acne, is irritating her to the point of causing a temper tantrum. The subject under discussion is little green men with big ears from Mars. Sabrina's close to screaming with rage.

Henry Buttershaw, what makes you think I'll believe your stories about little green aliens driving Volkswagens on the highway? What kind of self-delusion causes you to believe I'd trust the word of an alcoholic with only half a brain? I went to High School and did all the right things. I know a thing or two. I could have been Mr. Robshaw's of Robshaw fine meats and cheese's company secretary if I'd taken up his offer. Everybody in my neighbourhood said I had it in me.

Henry rises from this seat, makes a grab at Sabrina's large bosom.

Give me some of that! When you're hot and bad tempered I go all funny. Why are you trying to dodge me Sabrina? I know you like it.

Our little girl from the fancy diner's really angry now.

Why you unemployed son of a pig fucker from Alabama....who the hell do you think you are? I've a good mind to take a carving knife out of that drawer and cut your balls off. Garbage like you shouldn't be allowed fresh air.

Really?

Yes. I'm beginning to regret the day I picked you up at the bus station. Why do I always take pity on cute looking old men with skin problems? I've had enough. You're going to have to leave. Where's your suitcase?

Upstairs in the bedroom with my box of talking frogs. Did you feed the bullfrog with red spots on its back this morning? The fat ones get really annoyed if you don't feed them regularly.

It's the same with people. Carl Bottomley down at the diner always makes a fuss if he doesn't get his eggs, bacon and pancakes double quick. I'm always having to tear him off a strip. He's the fattest, meanest, most evil mouthed man in the country. Don't forget to take your clean underwear out of the machine before you leave.

You're serious? You really want me to go? Who the hell's going to fix that little car of yours when I'm gone? Who the fuck's going to make you a hot drink before you go to bed? I'm useful round here. Sorry about making a grab for your titties. It's the first time. Give me a break.

Suddenly, entirely without warning, the ceiling collapses burying Sabrina and Henry Buttershaw under a mountain of plaster, wood and leaping frogs. An eerie silence fills the room. Louis Armstrong scat sings his way through some banal show tune on a stereo somewhere in the far distance.
The author flings open the door of his room and shouts obscenities at nobody in particular. He loved Sabrina, but now she's dead. "This has all been for nothing," he says, forcing himself to calm down. "A blind man in a snowstorm could have done better."
Mr. Pumpkin arrives, his head aglow, his nose a bright red cherry. "Where are Charlene, Matthew Froginall and all the rest?" he asks, reaching cheekily across the table to pour himself a cup of cold tea.
 "Where are those silly ladies from old England?"
The author falls to his knees, tears of anguish down his face. "I really don't know," he whimpers. "I really don't know" and God gives him a vision of a flower-filled garden and his long dead brother wearing pyjamas and smoking a pipe, of a dancing frog and a Norwegian choir flashing their arses. The tears dry up.
Mr. Pumpkin commences a waltz with the gravy stained ghost of sweet Charlene. "We are but onions in a field of turnips," he says to her translucent grinning face, resisting the urge to wipe the spittle from her lips. "I would kiss you like the devil if I had the urge."
And the thwack and suck of Frau Gluwein in full sexual flight can be heard drifting across the rooftops.
 "Sounds like torture to me," whispers Charlene. "Is everybody happy?" shouts the author banging a saucepan with a wooden spoon to emphasise his words. A glittering, spluttering barrage of lights, red and gold and icy

white, dominates the early evening sky.

"Martians?" inquires Mr. Pumpkin. "About to arrive are they?"

The author reaches for a pullover, a sudden change in the temperature causing him to shiver and shake. "I might not be here in the morning," he says. "Other commitments could find me elsewhere. I do hope this world can cope with my absence."

With a single swipe of a calloused tiny hand, Mr. Pumpkin extinguishes the candle that lights his head.

Shouts of joy can be heard in the yard outside. It would take a million more words to explain everything. The effort is too much.

"Bray like donkeys," calls the author from a distant place.

We hear aeroplane noises. Departure will be difficult.

One or two of us will have heart attacks before it's all over.

ALAN'S SEARCH FOR TRUE LOVE

NIGHT

I'll write this in the manner of a rapper, a buzz brain with a woolly cap on talking into a tape machine in his little bedroom. I'll gesticulate, oscillate, self fornicate till the black angel shrouds me up and sends me half dead down the highway without end, past juke joints where thugs wear corsets, cast piggy eyes on anything vaguely female. It must be she I'm looking for, that memory reflected in slippery bathroom floors, bars of pungent yellow soap, giant cups of spiced up, milkless tea. She that persists in walking noisily around the inside of my head, rattling my lonely bed when I least expect it, farting to announce her arrival on scary winter nights. I'm confused by booze, loosened up, biting into a biscuit the size of the face of Big Ben.

"Hungry dear?" she inquires. But she isn't there. Frank Marriot, postman and possessor of the largest feet in our village, says she never existed in the first place. He keeps bringing back the letters I write to her, saying things like "You're out of your skull Alan, there's no Magdeburg Street in Rotherham and nobody's ever heard of a Felicity Warburton." I could kick him in his fat gut when he talks like that: Thank God for Johnny Walker whisky and the bite it gives me at the back of the throat. I couldn't sleep at all if I didn't have that comfort.

It's been a year or more since I last shagged somebody. Spotty Eileen from "The Jolly Turk" wasn't up to much. I had to close my eyes after I'd done it. When my pal Edgar Brown asked me how it was, I nearly broke down in tears. I wanted warm and tender love but didn't get it.

I'm scribbling this in the stock room at Fletcher's supermarket. Last night wasn't up to much (as you probably noticed). I wasn't able to pass on anything even vaguely uplifting. The depressing nature of my bachelor existence was written down for all to read. I shouldn't have eaten those big digestive biscuits. The crumbs went right up my arse. Mum always said, "Don't nibble in bed." How right the bony old monster was. Her words of wisdom have followed me round through the years. Everytime I expose my bare backside at the kitchen window I think of her. "Keep your rear end covered at all times," she used to say, every summer when I went camping with my cousins. I often wondered what she was getting at. Perhaps she thought a passing cow would take a lick at it in the night, that a big black crow would drop from some tree, pop in the tent and take a peck down the crack. I never worked out the mysteries of her mind.

Last week I built a stack of soup cans so high I began to marvel at my ingenuity, fleetness of mind and ability to balance our supermarket's products superbly well without any assistance from anybody. The manager called me into his office after my task was completed, was offensive and critical without any real reason. I hate the slicky pomaded pisspot more than I can properly express. I'd like to shove his Gucci trainers up his arse and burn his mother's seaside bungalow down. My creative know-how should be a boon to him. Why did he make me take the stack down?

I was reminded of the time the family cat pissed all over a Christmas crib I'd built in the living room. It broke my heart to dismantle it. I can still hear mother drunkenly saying, "The three Kings are sodden and baby Jesus has got his straw all wet," then laughing fit to burst. She was always insensitive after she'd had a few. Dad drunk a lot at weekends. I remember when he fell down in a snowstorm, lost his trilby hat in the river. I imagined the rats hitching a ride in it, floating downstream to the waterfall and their doom. Nature's darker side has always fascinated me. Watching our cat devour a mouse under the kitchen table was a childhood experience I'll never forget. I loved the way he bit off its head and spat it out. Mother screamed continuously for ten minutes when she spotted it. Dad slapped her around the face with a wet flannel to calm her down.

EARLY MORNING

There's a scratching at my bedroom window. Is it the big tree outside flapping its branches in the high wind, or is it the ghost of my Auntie Margaret trying to enter the room to recover the two stout porcelain bulldogs she so generously bequeathed me? Life, at one o'clock in the morning on a foul winter's night has an eerie feel to it. When I'm reading in bed, like now, I often hear the floorboards squeak, doors in the passage outside suddenly open and slam shut with great force. If the book's absorbing, I just ignore it. It's tedious and not worth the effort, I get up to investigate. Tonight is a night for mysterious scratching sounds. I'm going to put down my book (a volume of football greats and their family backgrounds) and meditate on peace, God's grace and Felicity Warburton. They that ignore the spiritual side of existence are doomed to an excess of inner turmoil. All of my family suffer from boils and small-scale (but irritating) skin rashes. My pondering on the deeper things in life has led to a reduction in my vulnerability to these horrors. I now have the skin of a healthy young baby for most of the year. Oh, here's Felicity (she's always the first to make an appearance when I meditate). Ah, she's indicating that she's changed her address and that I need new pair of slippers. How do I know this? Her image appears on a small T.V. set (rather dated in appearance, but functional) that materialises at the foot of my bed. When I concentrate hard, she never fails to show up. It's a miracle. I'm comforted by it. The stuff I experience in a drunken state (bed rattling, her noisy farts and the like) is simply a mirage. My real Felicity speaks to me in a sign language that only me and she knows about. Everything's in code. Everything's as private as we want it to be. I don't give a damn what Frank Marriot says. My Felicity lives. She's smiling at me now. The love in her eyes makes me want to build a dozen soup can stacks, ride to the top of Mt. Everest on a tricycle, walk on a tightrope in my bathing costume across the Cheddar Gorge with the whole of England looking on. She turns my brain into a powerhouse without limits, causes me to rap and rhyme like some hazy, dazy street urchin. Oh bingo bingo bongo, I'm in love, love, love. Pass me my hairpiece, I want to look twenty and in my prime again. I'll ask her to take a train tomorrow afternoon, to pack her bags and leave Rotherham forever. I know she can't take much more of that boyfriend of hers. I've heard tell he's got a piece of spare in Arkwright Street who covers his betting losses. I think it's disgusting. I'm convinced she'll find my hairy chest and readiness to buy a meal out now and then more rewarding.

DAY

I'm eating sandwiches in Fletcher's cramped canteen, watching two plump stock room girls stuff oversized beefburgers into their gaping, red-rimmed mouths. Life has no point when I see this kind of thing. I'm almost thirty-nine, reasonably good looking and believe I deserve better. I want to settle down, utilise my talents with watercolours and wrought iron, become a famous artist. My paintings have always had their admirers. Auntie Margaret said I was the Van Gogh of our village (this was after I completed a portrait of both her cats with a large vase of tulips) and would earn millions and millions of pounds. What an optimistic old spinster auntie was. It's a pity her vision came unstuck. I've been working for John Fletcher and co. for over ten years now without a glimmer of fame or glory. I find it sort of sad, but the nearest I've come to celebrity is when I had my name in the local paper after entering an apple tart eating contest. Dad was really pleased. "It's good to see the family mentioned in print," he said, "could be the first time it's happened since your Auntie Norah was put on probation for knocking out your cousin Derek." Ah, Norah, she was a formidable type. I've heard tell she once attended evensong at Canterbury Cathedral in a bikini for a bet. They don't breed women of her outstanding qualities these days. I blame it on the invention of the washing machine. Females don't get the exercise they used to. My Felicity's an exception though. She's got biceps like small footballs and thighs any professional rugby player would be proud of. It'll be fun to go for long walks together. I'm sure she'll set a cracking pace, provide a real test for this wooden leg of mine. Mind you, my incapacity has never been a drawback. I've been operating a part-time window cleaning business for many years now without any kind of accident occurring. Sometimes I wonder how I do it. And how did I lose my right leg, you might be asking? The cause was an unusually large fish - a pike I think - that leapt from the river and bit my ankle while I was fishing. The bite, unattended for three days, turned septic, resulting in severe blood poisoning. The poison spread rapidly. I've been one-legged for over ten years now. Felicity has always been sympathetic, thank God. When I first told her about my incapacity (if you can call it that) I expected her enthusiasm for me to falter. How wrong can one be? She immediately tried to fix a few small window-cleaning jobs for me in Rotherham - if I decided to visit. Proof to me that my false leg would never be a barrier to our relationship. She's the practical sort.

EARLY EVENING

A voice has just told me Frank Marriot's in love with Felicity, that he's been returning my letters all this year because he doesn't want her to read my words of deep affection. It's strange, but my beloved hasn't been her usual happy self (although I know she's made a convincing job of pretending) for some time now. It's Saturday tomorrow I might waylay him on his round, ask him some pertinent questions. An honest bachelor like myself shouldn't be made to suffer because of the lust of others. Marriot's got a bad record as a postman. Old Belshaw from flat 2B informs me he's been waiting for a parcel of sex aids for weeks now. What if that sly bastard's stolen them? He could be dashing over to Rotherham every so often and using them on my Felicity. Strong words might have to be used. Fisticuffs could be on the cards. I've just got up from the T.V. to make a cup of milky coffee. My head's a dazzle with bright pink and yellow lights, flashing images of Rocky Marciano's bleeding head, fuzzy movies of Felicity in the nude. The woman I love must be mine and mine alone. Yes, I'll take a day off work, challenge him to tell the truth. I'll put a stop to his hanky panky. What can he offer her anyway? A piece of currant cake at the post office Christmas party, a ride to Rotherham in a borrowed parcel truck, a chance to wear his postman's beret in a downpour? I can steal tinned food for her Alsatian puppy, offer a free choice of our new, fashionable tee shirt range, I've got prospects in higher management. What has he got? My potential genius in retail will stun the world one day. I can see me opening a chain of supermarkets, dazzling the general public with my range of toiletries (something particularly appealing to Felicity) and soft toys. People will fight to enter my well-stocked premises, purchases from my shops will be much prized and coveted. I won't tell Felicity about my suspicions concerning Marriot. I'm convinced she's an innocent where lustful, calculating men are concerned. A beautiful woman requires a caring man. I am he.

SATURDAY AFTERNOON

He started to scream when I hit him with the axe, howled so lustily I thought he'd bring out the neighbours. "What have I done Alan?" he raved, his voice much louder and higher than normal. "Is it your monthly newsletter from the aero modelling club of yours? Hasn't it arrived?" Poor stupid bastard, his attempts to pacify me didn't work at all. I knew he was guilty. I wasn't going to let him escape. My Felicity was being sexually abused on a regular basis, his postbag was probably crammed with condoms and prickly vibrators when I struck.

The whole business took about five minutes, and, as far as I remember, left him lying in a pool of blood at the junction of Newbury and Carshalton avenues. I'm tired now. The accuracy of everything I say is questionable. I sense an evil robotic force taking over my mind, my mouth, my toes, my ear lobes, the giant polka dot bandanna I've just wrapped round my head. I'm watching T.V. in the kitchen, staring at a football match, a battle of wills between men dressed as boys. Why are the players angry at each other? Why are the spectators dressed in potato sacks, conical paper hats and black rubber boots? Oh, what a pleasant surprise. Felicity's out there, and she's waving at me! Has there ever been a more beautiful human being? Funny to see her at a football match though. That goalkeeper bears a startling resemblance to my old friend Edgar Brown. Strange, now she seems to be smiling in his direction. I'll call on him tonight after the game, ask a few relevant questions. Maybe there's more to her smile than meets the eye?

OCCURRENCES

The night a giant sausage emerged from the sea I was boiling my underpants. It wasn't a job I enjoyed, in fact it was work that diminished my self worth, frequently led me to mope unnecessarily in front of my girlfriend. I'm a world renowned tester of leather waistcoats, oversized beach balls and rubber bones for dogs and my phone never stops ringing, causing Mabel, the able girlfriend I've just mentioned, to go into a spin. "Why do they always want you?" she frequently complains, revealing a deep-rooted jealousy she's unable to control. "What's so special about an undersized underpants boiler who spends his time queening about in fancy waistcoats, biting rubber dog bones and jumping up and down on garishly coloured beach balls? I went to Belfast University and nobody wants me for anything."
The problem with highly qualified types is they expect a rich reward for their self-serving efforts. I could have been the headmaster of my local girls school if I'd studied harder. Do I make myself clear on this point or am I heading for the steaming swamps of confusion again?

"I'm a Zealot," he said, as he handed me a large whip and ordered me to thrash myself. All thoughts of sausages, sea, and rubber bones for dogs departed from my fevered brain. It was a February morning; cold, misty in the garden. It was the weather for sad birds to sing sad bird songs. I took the whip and commenced the beating. "Harder," he screeched, his fireman's helmet slipping over his eyes, plunging him into darkness he was never to recover from. I thought I deserved the self-abuse. His screeching was the screeching of a jackdaw in hell. I understood it more than anything I've ever understood. When I left him, my naked back a mess of blood and tattered flesh, he was struggling to remove the helmet from his head, cursing the world and its doubtful wonders to high heaven. I could have helped him but I didn't. A dozen fat beach balls awaited my attention. I hadn't the time.

Nor had I the time for the unctuous attentions of a papal delegate who arrived on my doorstep one wet Wednesday morning. I threw his brochures into the gutter, almost debagged him as I forced him down on the slippery pavement. "What right have you to do this?" he yelled, as I thrust my knee into his nose. Then I heard the flutter of crazed wings in my head, imagined beaks pecking at the rotting corpse of a bug-infested rabbit. I realised I would have to force myself to stop, but couldn't do it. It took a rosy-cheeked postman with an appalling breath problem to drag me off him. "Steady on fatty," was all I heard as I blacked out. I had no time to chew on rubber bones for dogs, bounce up and down on beach balls or wear outrageous waistcoats for weeks afterwards. The employment exchange, doubtful of the validity of my work from day one (whenever that was), refused to pay me a single penny in benefits. Everything that happened simply confirmed my status as one of God's outsiders.

The evening an oversized crab sat at the foot of my bed and demanded to discuss the works of Marcel Proust, I was dreaming about ironing my shirts and taking a long holiday with the butcher's boy in Barbados. I heard the boy's lilting voice, "Take the steaklets," it said, "select suitable sausages" and felt myself smile. Then I became aware of the crab. He wore a peaked cap; held a pencil and paper in one of his twitching pincers, asked if I could speak French. "Non," was the best I could manage, images of powdered prostitutes, drugged and helmeted cyclists forming in my mind as I said it. It was an embarrassing admission to make, one that caught me reddening at the cheeks, breaking wind nervously. The pincers snapped at my nose, tweaked and tweaked till the blood dripped, as the crab decided to punish me for my ignorance. I'm now noseless at the weekends. The night with the crab resulted in dark magic that appears to be permanent. I've given up visiting the cinema on Saturday nights. To be as I am, abnormal beyond the point of reason, is a difficult role to play. It's most shaming.

Now back to Mabel (remember she's my girlfriend) and her multitude of problems.
A conversation – some time in the middle of last week:

Mabel!

Yes dear.

Are we ever to marry, to have babies, to live as Fotheringay and that slag of wife of his live?

My depression regarding the future of my soul probably stems from this. Is it Buddhists who roll up their trousers when they're being irritated?

No dear, I think it's Mellish from number thirty three and his order of dragons. His wife's a dragonette you know, always wears a purple dressing gown on their annual seaside holiday.

For bathing?

No, for washing the dishes, polishing the lino – that sort of thing.

So where is it, what is it, how am I to do it? The peace I seek seems beyond my grasp, slips from my hands like wet socks in the washtub. Once I thought Father Christmas had paid me a visit but it turned out to be Mum dressed up in a beard and red anorak. Am I to be fooled for the rest of my life?

Probably. I missed out on a brand new pair of earrings when Desmond, probably the most generous boyfriend I ever had, died before his time. It was my birthday and he was on his way to see me when he collapsed in the street. I emptied his pockets in the hospital but couldn't find anything. I'm sure they were stolen.

You haven't had much luck in your life have you?
Didn't you almost lose your leg in a climbing accident once?

Yes, I fell off a small Welsh mountain while trying to pass a fellow climber a sandwich. The rescue team were most kind. I almost married the big bearded one with the bobble hat and snazzy pullover.

I laugh till I fart at times. Conversations with my Mabel frequently take a weird, wonderful and smelly turn. What I've just recounted to you is typical of our chats together. I've got a terrific memory for it. I don't forget a single thing. Sometimes the beach balls burst when I'm testing them (I'm changing the subject because I'm getting bored. Do you mind?) Large explosions occur, neighbours stick their heads out of bedroom windows to observe and complain. "Stop that fucking row," might say one. "Can't you do that in a field somewhere," might shout another.

Working in ones back garden can be a precarious business, particularly on a council estate. The lack of privacy is intimidating.
I'm prone to strange occurrences, have a fear of senility (I'm approaching sixty) and levitate more than is good for me. If you feel a shadow passing over the roof of your house after midnight it's probably me. Levitation releases me from the stress of the day. Spicy foods can bring on a spontaneous bout of it as well. Last night I couldn't remember my brother's name when he called me about a motorbike and sidecar he was intending to purchase. This kind of incident often sets off a fit of anxiety, has me pacing around in the backyard till I become dizzy. No wonder the neighbours call me Dizzy Dennis (although my real name's Edgar), no wonder they call the police when I fall into the hedgerow, start to scream. "He's a danger to himself," I've heard them say. They could be right.

I failed in the meat trade, couldn't tell a lamb chop from a medallion of fine pork. My enthusiasm was undeniable though. John Hoggis, master of all things dead flesh in this ancient town of ours, still vouches for my veracity today. "Edgar could have been serving behind that counter," he'll always say when he spots me shopping in the butchers, "all he lacked was a thorough knowledge of the goods he was trying to sell."

My entrance into the world of waistcoats, beach balls and rubber bones for dogs is sometimes hard to explain. The world needs people to try out and test things; maybe I'm just a natural choice for this kind of job. When I applied for my position with the rubber bones people the boss asked to inspect my false teeth. Some, and I know plenty who would have been, might have been offended. I wasn't. I took it as a logical step towards becoming a capable, bone biter. I've never regretted my action. And the beach balls? Well, it's quite an exhausting job for a sixty year old, but I like it. The company, also noted for their production of rubber rings, beach huts and watering cans, have always been generous with their free samples. I've more watering cans in my garden shed than any man I know. Avril got me into the waistcoat business. "You've got just the belly for it," she said one day after I took my shirt off to make love to her in the kitchen. "It's prominent enough to test the sturdiest of fabric." Pity about Avril. She lost her heart to a rugby player form South Australia, gave up making waistcoats and took up full-time sex. What a waste of an active mind.

I bought Mabel a new kitchen table last Christmas. "Think of the stuff I can stack on it," she said gleefully as she unwrapped it. "Onions, extra large cabbages, giant bottles of vino, hundreds of potatoes, just about anything...." I laughed till my stomach ached. Her pleasure tickled my fancy no end. And it was the same when I treated her to a change of hairstyle at Master Roger's. She almost wept when she looked in the mirror that evening, saying things like, "It's the most beautiful beehive I've ever had" and "I could meet the Queen looking like this." Mabel, despite her petty jealousies and lack of sound computer skills, is essential to my current existence. Her backside would win major awards if competitions took place. I like the cheeks firm, round and super large. She fits the bill perfectly.

The night the second giant sausage emerged from the sea I was eating pickled onions and cheddar cheese in bed. The foaming brine could hardly contain itself; bubbling, burping, it almost flooded the seafront. Our local paper printed a lurid account of the landing the next day. The headline: "Sausage full of illegal immigrants lands at two in the morning," was both incorrect and sensational, as the sausage was only half full of immigrants and the time of arrival was closer to midnight than two. I want accurate reportage when I read my newspaper. "The Bumbleton Echo" has been nothing but a lying gossip sheet since it was first published. The giant sausage business confirmed this.

When the dwarf Harold Crowley was killed by an exploding beach ball I was almost persuaded to form a trade union. My telephone conversation with his widowed wife, which I'll relay to you in a second, was both sad and revealing. Harold, a midget shot-putt champion, was a man of outstanding abilities. His death, caused by excess air in a shoddily welded ball, was avoidable. Here's part of my long chat with Edna Crowley:

Sorry to hear about Harold's untimely demise Edna, what have you done with his dart trophies, his tiger skin leotard, the special heavy leather boots with the thick rubber soles he always wore when testing?

I've sent them to his mother. She's got a glass cabinet in her living room she's going to put them in. Did you know we're burying him in the back garden? We've got special permission from the council.

Am I invited to the funeral? I'll rush out immediately and purchase a new suit if I am.

Of course Edgar. Harold always spoke highly of you, frequently said your abilities with beach balls was second to none. He also admired your taste in short trousers.
Do you still like them in leather, and tight? I repeat, your prowess in all things beach ball is a legend throughout the ball-testing world. It would be an honour to have you along.

I'll be there then. When and where does the sad event take place?

It's at the Ethiopian Baptist Church in Longmore Street at ten o'clock on Saturday morning. Wally Bush from the Bouncy Bouncy Beach Ball Co should be attending. I'll be making an appointment with him to check out compensation afterwards. I think I should be amply rewarded for Harold's death.

My goodness Edna, you're quick off the mark. I don't blame you though. Life without Harold's regular income is going to be tough.

Enough is enough. The conversation with Edna Crowley wasn't as interesting as I thought it was. I thought she talked in detail about his illustrious shot-putt career, his outstanding collection of Victorian footwear, his stalwart stand against corruption in the rabbit breeding business. My memory of our talk together, which I taped for posterity, has turned out to be pathetic. What bores we both were.

Mabel wants to marry me. I'm not sure about it at all. I'd like to remain footloose and fancy free, available to all the young creatures (there's a blonde in the rubber bone distribution centre I particularly like at the moment) I have an interest in. I know I'm old but I don't care. Why shouldn't a man with my distinctive looks share his bed with some young sweetie? Sex is good for the brain, adds strength and purpose to a life like mine. I'm not ready for so called marital bliss, regular supermarket shopping, sharing household tasks on a daily basis. And in any case, what woman would seriously want to live with a man whose nose tends to vanish at the weekend? Mabel doesn't know about my difficulty because I always tell her I've got a large order of bones to bite into on Saturdays and Sundays. The deception can't last forever though. One day she's going to pay me a surprise visit and find me utterly noseless doing the washing up. I have nightmares about it.

The night God almost decided to put an end to things I was watching three of my neighbours ascending to heaven clutching the tails of snorting winged pigs. They were such vociferous beasts; madly flexing their trotters they put up a hell of a fight to stay on solid ground. The energy force from above, however, was too much for them. I believe God had urgent business with my neighbours in heaven and the pigs were subjected to divine gravitational pull. It's always best to give in to God. But what would mere pigs know about this?

I've a fierce desire to go to Hollywood and star in a major film production (sorry, I'm changing the subject again but I just have to get this out), something like Titanic or a Harry Potter epic. The desire to dress in strange clothes and play a part is overwhelming. My regular day-to-day wear, jeans and sensible sports jacket, conspires to make me feel ordinary, which I'm not. Modelling the exotic waistcoats, a job that happens fairly infrequently these days, is some kind of compensation, but not enough. I want to dress in finery: brocaded uniforms, tall silk hats, boots of the finest soft leather that reach the thighs. The dowdy dude I appear to be is not me. I'm more than a legend in my own lunch break. I admired Rod Steiger when he played the part of Al Capone. What a forceful, mean spirited little bastard he was. My God, the way he curled those lips, intimidated everybody with his menacing stare. It's a role I could play. I think I'll write to one of the Hollywood bigwigs, see if they'll have me. I can imagine the telephone conversation when the chief of productions rings to tell me to fly over to L.A. and take a film test. I'm sure it goes something like this:

Hello, is that the rubber bone biter from Bumbleton on Sea, the guy who sent me the photos of himself dressed as a gangster?

Yes, it is.

Good, my name's Max Roebuck, I'm the director of productions at Fantastika Films. I'm glad I caught you in.

Me too.

Yes...well...I think you have a future on the silver screen, but not as that bastard Capone. You have a kind face. I imagine you as a chubby alien sent to earth to save the Amazon rain forests, the kind of guy who walks into a diner one day and buys everybody a blueberry muffin.

Why a muffin?

Because all aliens like to buy earthlings things. I once heard of one in Nebraska who bought a farmer a tractor. Aliens always try to make friends. Being green and having enormous ears is a hell of a poor start in life. They have to try harder.

Whoa, wait a minute. I'm not sure I want to be green and have big ears. And this business about being chubby! I want to present myself to the public at my slimmest and best. I've lost weight recently.

Really? What a shame. We'd like you to be as fat as fat can be. I've also thought of you as a plump strawberry in a film we're about to make about fruit life in a farmer's market. Would you mind being dyed red and wearing a fluffy green wig? It's that amiable face of yours. Could you imagine a singing, talking strawberry, one that falls in love with a cherry and lives happily ever after?

I can imagine their children.

Can you? That's a start. You're obviously right for the part. I'll send your ticket over in the next few days. Goodbye Edgar. Stardom awaits you.

What if it all came true?
I can see my Mabel on my arm at my first great film premier, hear the voices of the cheering crowd.
"ADOLPHO," they're calling, "Adolpho" (I'll have changed my name for artistic reasons by then). Then our limousine arrives, we step in.

Most of the fans in the crowd are dressed as strawberries. I'm a big influence on all of their boring lives...Oh the fantasies I have, the little explosions of wonderment I conjure up to brighten up the days. I could have been a writer of some consequence. Mabel says my handwriting is that of a man of supreme honesty and intelligence. She's an expert at this kind of thing. I've perused some of the learned books she's read on the subject.

Last night I levitated above an angry sea full of super giant sausages. "What is the meaning of all of this?" I heard myself screaming above the whistling, howling mind. "What am I being told? What significance do these plump objects have in relationship to the future of the world?" My pyjamas were soaking wet when I woke. Had it been such a warm night? It was early in the morning. I went downstairs to my cramped kitchen to make a cup of tea. Basil, Mabel's little Pekinese dog who I'd been taking care of over the weekend, yapped and sniffed at my smelly feet as I boiled the kettle. "Fuck off you little Chinese twat," I shouted, revealing that nasty racist side of myself I was always trying to conceal. My mind was full of sausages stuffed with immigrants, interlopers, invading armies from other planets. I certainly wasn't at my best.

I've written all this in an effort to convince the world I have special qualities. I'm not normal. I don't want to be. Within me is the power of re-organise the whole infrastructure of Bumbleton on Sea, solve the mystery of the giant sausages and star in a Hollywood blockbuster.
I'm almost sixty and my life, fascinating in all its many and varied details, is a closed book to most of you. This all has to change. I'm of the belief that all I've achieved could be to the greater good of mankind. I need a publicity agent; in fact I met up with one in my local pub the other day. Here are some of the things we said:

Publicity, is it Edgar, the desire to be known beyond the realms of our quaint little town? It would be better if you'd murdered somebody or played as a reserve striker for some obscure third division football club. Who on earth's interested in a well rounded nobody who bites rubber dog bones for a living?

And occasionally models embroidered waistcoats at Bradley's in the

High Street!

So what Edgar! And all this stuff about testing beach balls. I'm surprised you haven't slipped and twisted an ankle at your age. When are you going to give it all up?

When I get my big Hollywood break. I've sent letters off to all the relevant parties. Mr. Spielberg should be contacting me soon. I'd make a marvellous Mr. Pickwick. Do you know they're thinking of remaking the old Dickens classic? Brad Pitt might be starring in it.

With you? Ernest, you're going crazy. What does Mabel think of all of this?

She wonders why I'm always working overtime at the rubber dog bone factory at weekends.

And why is that?

Because my nose mysteriously disappears on Saturdays and Sundays and I don't want her to see this. It's because of a bad tempered crab. The horrible creature put a spell on me.

Have you seen a doctor about the problem – a priest, a psychic! Why this great urge to be known everywhere? If I was you I'd want to keep my secrets to myself. Any more odds and ends in your ragbag of horrors?

Well, there's my intermittent conflict with an agent of the Catholic Church, the inner compulsion to be flogged now and then, my visions of giant sausages tumbling from the sea on to our pristine beaches, the time I almost became the best butcher in town....

Can you carve a sheep up, produce chops to make the mouth water? And those sausages. Are the ones you imagine pork or beef?

Hard to tell. They mostly arrive in the dark.

Sad, sad, sad. Edgar, all I can do is make public your tendency to go nuts now and then. Who's interested? The world's crammed to the top with nowhere men like yourself. Now if you were Fiona Bullivant, that would be something.

Why?

Genius Edgar, the ability to design garments that the general public rush to purchase. Fiona's got it. She's making a CD soon as well. I'm escorting her to her first recording session next week. She's a singer.

I've never heard of her. Is she local?

Indeed she is, my daughter-in-law in fact. I first discovered her knitting in the back kitchen one Wednesday afternoon. The colours she used on that pullover were outstanding. I encouraged her to graduate to the scissors, to cutting and stitching together beautifully shaped shirts and jackets. My house is full of her clothes waiting for buyers. The telephone rings a lot.

Can she sing? You say she's making a CD, but can she really sing? Most of them are useless when it comes down to it.

She certainly can. She knows everyone of Celine Dion's tunes backwards. I'm going to put her together with assembled African drummers and a string quartet. It should be interesting.

I hope so too, for your sake. You'll be the laughing stock of this pub when I hit the big time. You're missing out on a great chance. I almost feel sorry for you.

Little Basil and the ever-faithful Mabel were waiting for me when I arrived home. Basil shit on my slippers as I prepared a light supper, but I hardly noticed. Depression kills the fire inside. Mabel looked pale and concerned as we sipped at our soup. The publicity man and his negativity would take a lot of recovering from.

The day a giant beach ball engulfed the town hall I was playing dominoes with Mabel.

"Edgar, we need your help," said a nervous policeman on the phone shortly after the awful event.
"We need your expertise. Come quick, the mayor's trapped in his office with his elderly secretary."
I dashed to the scene only to find the situation under control and a solitary rotund policeman on guard outside the mayor's office.
"Where's the beach ball?" I inquired. "And what's the mayor up to so late in the afternoon?"
"Fucking," replied the officer, his face glowing with embarrassment as he spoke. "He's got his secretary under the desk and, from what I hear, they're both thoroughly enjoying themselves."
"And the ball?" I asked. "How come there's not a trace of it anywhere? Who took it away?"
"Oh that was the enormous flying alligator from Moscow zoo, he just took it up in his jaws and flew off with it," answered the agitated fatty.
I was mystified and annoyed. I bit a rubber bone clean in two at work that evening. Anger makes me bite harder. The misuse of my time by incompetent officialdom has always been one of my pet hates.

"Why are we all so fat?" asked Mabel over dinner last Tuesday. "Don't know," I mumbled, mouth full, a bowl full of gherkins distracting me considerably.
"Let me finish these and I'll tell you." But I never did. The conversation moved on to other themes and all talk of obesity was forgotten.
As I approach my sixtieth year I wonder what the point of it all is.
Would life have been a little more interesting if I'd made a success of butchery, opened my own shop and become a black pudding specialist? Ah the sausages.
Am I to be forever harassed by these gigantic lumps full of people, the swirling sea, crabs with devilish claws, flying pigs?
I'm looking in the mirror at my noseless face as I write. It's Saturday and I'm utterly alone. I'm talking to myself, asking and replying:

So Edgar, where does it all go from here?

To the beach balls. I've got some overtime testing to do tomorrow.

Sunday! You work on Sunday?

Yes, it's to keep Mabel away. I think I've already told you about it. I'd hate her to see my face without a nose.

I understand, but isn't it difficult? Doesn't she get suspicious?

She does, but I ignore her. Little Basil gets all her love and attention when I'm unavailable. She takes him for walks by the river (where he's often savaged by larger dogs), has his coat trimmed regularly. Then there are her computer skills. She's trying to improve them at the moment. She's looking for a job, something in the top executive range.

Ambitious!

Absolutely. She went to Belfast University, played hockey for three seasons, developed that muscular figure of hers. Yes, she's ambitious.

And yourself?

I think I'm giving up on all of that. My position as an upright member of society is under question.
Lord Horatio Nelson keeps visiting me and asking me to go carp fishing with him. Sometimes I can't believe what I'm seeing. Neighbours are talking. They want to know who the small man in the knee breeches, white stockings, black eye patch and funny hat is. Don't they know? Where's their sense of history? Surely they must have heard of Lady Hamilton and the great admiral, of his fornicating with her on a billiard table?

Oh, I didn't know he played. I'll challenge him to a match next time he's round. Bare buttocks on the green baize. Makes you think doesn't it? She must have been something special?

Like me. I'm special.

Like me too. I'm special.

Is that the wind whistling through the trees? Is that a big blue sausage floating above the house? Soon the back garden will be full of beach balls. How I wish I had more space for my work. Life on a post-war council estate can get awfully cramped. I need somewhere like Buckingham Palace gardens to test the balls in. All that space wasted. I just might write to Her Majesty.

About your balls?

About life, about crabs who steal noses, about my failure to convince the world of my singular role in things.

Sleep…

Can't.

And why not?

Because the engines of the night are already beginning to whirr. Things are on the move. Cats are already crackling their way through the dry, dead grass. If I sleep I'll miss the crab's visit, miss the action if he decides to pluck off my ears. I want to be awake. I want to know if I'm to be deaf to the world.

What a horror.

What a scenario God gives us.

The old fool.

A TRUE FRIEND

Old nobbly spotty nose, ally to all who would seek a smile on a wet and wintery day. I'm pleased to know him, to call him friend, to pay my taxes so that people like he can carry on. Saturday afternoon in the city centre shopping precinct wouldn't be Saturday afternoon without old Nobbyspots (that's my special name for him) doing his thing. What a dancer he is! What a singer and harmonica player! It's a pleasure to hand him a few shillings after a performance, pat him on his hunched back, beg and plead for an encore. It makes my weekend.
Oh the fun we have.
"Give us another tune," I'll shout. "Must rest," he'll say. "One more time." I'll shout, louder. "Not yet," he'll mutter, breathless. And so on, and so on, until he finally gives in.
It's almost a ritual. I haven't missed a Saturday for over two years.
And it's almost always the same number for the encore, "Girl from Ipanema." My God, it's a beautiful, haunting, melodic piece.
I can almost see the girl's big arse wobbling in a mild Brazilian breeze when he sings it. He has the ultimate rough but tender vocal chords.
I wonder if he smokes. My girlfriend keeps my company regularly on my city visits. Nobbyspots isn't her style, though.
"I like a proper singer in a proper concert hall," she'll always say when I ask her opinion of the performance. "A fat street singer in a dirty vest and smelly overcoat doesn't move me in the slightest."
Three weeks ago I asked Nobbyspots to sing something by Celine Dion.
"I don't know any yuppie songs;" he said, grimacing.
I felt let down, and told him so.
His reply was to take out his not inconsiderable penis and flap it at me threateningly. A highly irate member of the public called a policeman over. Nobbyspots was arrested, immediately.

Guilt seeped from my every pore afterwards. I couldn't sleep for two nights. There was a short piece in the paper yesterday about Nobbyspots in court; my girlfriend pointed it out to me over coffee in the office.
"I didn't know his real name was Derek Raspberry," she snickered.
I almost joined in but controlled myself. His sentence (six months in prison for exposing himself and striking a police officer) seemed just a fraction excessive. Old Nobbyspots Raspberry (the papers say he's fifty-

five) is a man who's given me so much pleasure.
Oh I'll miss our weekly visits to watch him perform. I wonder if he's learning some new material in prison?
My ever cynical girlfriend is sceptical about this. "He's too lazy to learn anything modern and fresh," is all she has to say on the subject. I'm not so sure. With his powerful voice he would do well to get into the blues a little more, tackle some big ballads.
I wonder if he's got a CD player in his cell?

ALIVE

He can't breath.
He's changed. His flesh has turned a yellow custard colour, his eyes a deep sea green. The lack of air doesn't bother him though. Another state of being is taking over. A chorus of saxophones serenade him from an imagined distant hill. He has a feeling that Louis Armstrong will greet him when he gets to wherever he's going. The hiss, puff, hiss of a steam train gives the impression of a journey taking place. Someone calls out for tickets to be shown. "Sounds like Grandpa Bartlett," he hears himself saying. He can't feel his tongue. All his teeth seem to have vanished.

There's a small room with beautifully made stained glass windows, large oil paintings of donkeys wearing crowns, fierce ravens in police helmets. He turns to an invisible companion who smells strongly of onions, barks out, "What is the purpose of this ordeal? Are we to be forever kept in the dark?" It's then he realises he's talking out of his arse and that his sphincter hurts. Two fat ducks fly to the left of him. "Careful where you're going," he says with great difficulty.

He's always hoped to hear God's voice just before passing over, something reassuring like, "You don't need a soap and towel where you're going Ron." There hasn't been so much as a whisper. The fact that he's now reduced to talking out of his backside is leading to a crisis of confidence. "Do you talk out of your arse as well?" he inquires of another invisible presence floating somewhere underneath where he imagines his body to be. "Is your shit hole sore?" "No," says an upper class voice with a breath that reeks of garlic and cigarette smoke. "My orifice is as it always was. I communicate out of a bunghole in the top of my head. It corks itself up when it isn't in use."
He wants to ask how but the presence removes itself. His new existence leaves little time for prolonged contact.

Now he feels his eyes revolving in their sockets, his nose starting to swell to an enormous size. "I'll be the laughing stock of Mobbet's and Co," he says to nobody in particular, "if I ever return."
A vision of his office desk suddenly fills his mind. A fat stranger in a red wig appears to be using his computer. "My God, they've soon got a new

man in," he blubbers, imagining tears but not feeling them. "It's hard work and profit above all things at that rotten firm. I was always too sensitive for those greedy bastards." The soreness and irritation from his talking arse worsens.

His thoughts turn to happier moments, Carol and himself playing tennis one Sunday in the autumn twilight. "I wonder if she talks out of her backside as well," he thinks to himself. But then he has to laugh, causing himself further discomfort. His condition is becoming a bore.

"I'm Sir Stanley Matthews, football wizard and committed naturist," shouts a voice somewhere to what seems to be his left. Sadly, a howling wind suddenly develops, causing the great man's voice to become unintelligible. All he can hear are the words 'trickery', 'juggling' and 'toilet paper'. "Why don't you keep your gusting and blustering out of my life," screams the unhappy, subject of this tale to the wind. "Sir Stanley and I could have swapped football stories. I could have asked him why he always wore such long shorts."

The wind, surprisingly, replies. "Long live the King," it puffs deeply, masterfully. "May his spotty face get better, his urine take on a clarity associated with the purest of spring waters." Our lost and confused one, while mindful of the delicate state of his backside, holds forth with cautious venom. "Who the hell is this King you refer to? Does he have a throne, a palace, an aviary where he keeps exotic birds? Can he ride a horse bareback? I was a man with a profound sense of logic before I came here. Nonsense begets nonsense. What on earth am I talking about?"

The wind grows silent.

A flock of crisp, dry leaves turn, twist and fall. Great chunks of the past invade his mind. His whole being (or what remains of it) feels itself being kicked to oblivion. The robbery and murder on that country lane comes to life. He, the victim, gasps with anger, deep sorrow and pain. "Too real," he howls. "Too real."

"Is that you Jeremy?" he calls to a passing grey form, his distress subsiding almost immediately. "I think I recognise that strong soap you use to fight body odour. Are you naked?" "No, I'm not Jeremy," answers the grey form, tetchily. "I'm Toby Crippen, long lost nephew of the famous murderer. Have you just arrived here?" Our murdered soul (for that's

what he appears to be) is puzzled, remains silent for some length of time. The mysterious grey shadow that claims to be related to a notorious wife killer from the early part of the twentieth century continues:
"Dear person, once I had a job in a large department store, sold deck chairs and oversized trunks to travellers. Mine was a most pleasant existence. I occasionally got to undress rich young ladies." Our beleaguered one interrupts, shouts loudly. "I don't want to hear tales of sexual depravity, seedy little nonsense about breast fondling and underwear removing. Every word you've uttered is a lie. I was killed for my watch and an empty wallet. There must be someone in this somewhere who can offer comfort, friendship, advice. Mad nonsense about Crippen and department stores doesn't help at all." A shoal of dying fish flashes by. Louis Armstrong sings 'Wonderful World' to a wretchedly unsuitable backing. The grey form vanishes without a trace. Our man is alone with his shattered mind. He has to adapt somehow.

"It's time for a song," says a voice from a cavern in a mountain he can't visualise. "Know anything by Schubert? Can you sing in German?"
"No," he mumbles, just a tiny bit intimidated by the loud echo on the voice. "I can't remember the words to a single song. My teacher at school said I had the most tuneless voice he'd ever heard."
There's a clatter of saucepans, the sound of someone sucking on a straw. "Delicious," says another voice, smacking its lips. "Delicious, delicious, delicious. Tomato soup with a hint of parsley has always been a favourite of mine. Mother used to make it regularly before she left us and moved to Manchester." And so they rattle on.
Voices from the dark, voices from false daylight, voices from the boots and socks and arse. And will he discover why and when and who the murderer was? Will it matter anyway after his arse has worked itself to a speechless standstill?
"Happy holidays," he calls out to the rattle, bangs and clangs that surround him. No one answers. A sharp beak pecks at his ragged, damaged left ear. The moves towards a conclusion are being made as he drifts.

DAYS BY THE SEA

I'm your little firework. I explode, sparkle; fornicate with the winter sky. "Caress my soul," you murmur, "make play with my senses." I try, but words splutter out before actions. "It's the barmy eyed poet in you," you bluster, sniffling a bit.

Pause. Think. Describe:

We have a room on the same corridor. Drunken members of this therapeutic community of ours frequently defecate by our doors. At meetings in the orange painted refectory we protest. "Billy shit in front of Mildred while I was hoovering up," you say, screeching with indignation. Bleached blond Derek, noted troublemaker and one of the most brazen shitters around, laughs. I find myself reaching for his neck to strangle him. Tall nurses prevent me.

And how, you might ask, did we get here?

In a blistering hurry stuck in gleaming pink perambulators pushed by fussy pushy mothers wearing plaid skirts, sensible shoes, knitted hats. In wooden Spitfires piloted by snooty pilots hurtling fast across landscapes strewn with nappies. "You could see the shit stains from the air," you gigglingly remember after I remind you of it all. But laughable it certainly wasn't. Criminal though - certainly.

I'm your baby jolly boy stuck fast to your whims till you tell me otherwise. You shout "fetch the crayons for picture making" and I scamper about till all is prepared. This kiddo seeks to please, would break wind at a papal gathering if you so wished.

And does God help us?

A crucifix hangs over the bed in every room. Five saintly priests visit our establishment in rotation. Cocksucking is forbidden during waking hours. We take our pills and dwell upon the afterlife. We apply ourselves to all therapies with a diligence that astounds the casual visitor. Who amongst you in that outside world of yours could live as we do? It takes discipline and order to thwart the devils within. That horned beast of a being has no place on our tennis courts and football fields.

Pause. Think. Try to relax.

The sea is close by. On designated happy days we're allowed to frolic on the sands. Your love is at its best when active during these periods. You become playful; slip my heavy denim overalls to my knees, smother my pubic hairs with fine sand. The sun (if it's out and in the mood to give succour) never fails to add a magic to the proceedings. "And a good time was had by all" are words our supervisors use frequently at the conclusion of these fun occasions. We are then stared at meaningfully, required to nod in agreement. I, personally, never have problems performing this simple physical task. Days by the sea are always a thrill.

Change. Adjust. Compromise?

If being part of your society means wearing froggy glasses and pip popping away at a computer keyboard you can count me out.

WITH MARIA BY THE SEA

I feel fresh, my juices rising, my little cock singing.
Maria come play your harp on the balcony, place your rump on this finest of seats, and play. And the sea, the blue blue sea, what a friend it is to little old me. It is I who befriend seagulls, pittlediddled old ladies in dangerous dark bars; it is I Madame, it is I.
This summer was loincloth weather, the stuff of Tarzan and co.
It was perfect for burglary as well; plenty of dark, warm nights, not a lot of moonlight. Maria, may I ask for your hand in glorious ejaculation? The road to Sodom is not far ahead, bright yellow shoots of fire light the night sky. Dear dog of dogs how I'd love to doggy doggy you now. Would you twang at your harp while I pretend I'm William Burroughs taking notes? How innocent you wish you were. Surely you know of beaky nosed Bill Burroughs, every little girl's horrible lollipop man? I'm here to tell you he was gay Madame, wouldn't have harmed a pimple on your hairless arse. "But to penetrate," you say, "that is surely the thing."
I feel I must slap your face for the impudent nature of your remarks but desist. A little voice tells me your innocence is probably quite genuine. Oh this wondrous sea air, our balcony with a splendid view, the sheer excellence of the surroundings. Oh how it serves to soothe the potential evil in me, turn my ears into teddy bear ears, my nose into a raspberry coloured button. Maria, the mirage, the lustrous goal; you that make the squeals when all I want is serious passion.
A question: When the harp playing is over will you allow me to wrestle with you a little, disturb the thick pile I hoovered so carefully today? To be sure I'm a little overweight of late, but will you?
The sea roars and...oh she's fallen in a dead faint by the bookcase.
Have I frightened her with my loose talk (for loose talk it will certainly be seen as if this ever gets to a court of law)? The lustful nature of my recent self has surprised me.
I thought it was buried years ago along with the shrivelled condoms at the bottom of my underwear drawer. Her little harp and she may have to be dropped off the balcony if she doesn't recover rapidly. This is a strange and compelling set of circumstances. Oh to be told that all is well, that I've ceased to be a dirty minded old sinner.
I dream. I dream. When Maria wakes she could scream, run to the hall-

way, call the police. I do not want this. Inspector Freebody has hauled me over the coals more than once before. Sergeant Cockerill has my name in several of his little leather-bound notebooks. Another encounter with either of them could lead to a prison sentence of some length. Oh curses on the pervert within me that makes me make so many naughty suggestions to the young ladies. It's the kind of disease all music teachers should be extremely wary of. I need to see a good psychiatrist, spill out my all on his couch.

Friends (the few that I have these days) have been advising me to seek help for ages. Even my ex-wife's been ringing and counselling caution. Oh thank God. Maria's just opened her eyes and requested a glass of water. Her lips appear to be a little blue but the rest of her looks as enchanting as ever. Blue lips and a pale green mini dress – most fetching.

Long live the timid light of lust within me. I mean no harm.

Ah, she speaks. What is it dear? Do you wish to retire to the bathroom and splash a little cold water on those pasty cheeks of yours?

I'll make some tea and toast while you attend to it.

MY LIFE WITH RONALD AND OTHERS

We are nothing. We are balloons drifting in a light wind towards a prickly bush. Ronald, he of the fattest arse in the history of mankind, recently told me he's going to work on a farm somewhere in Uganda. "I'll miss you," I said, as we shared a pizza with Big Miriam from the flat below us. "Me too," purred the big one, a piece of tomato slithering down her hairy chin. Ronald wants to grow maize, help feed the starving. "Why you?" I asked as we prepared for bed. "We are nothing. We are balloons drifting in a light wind towards a prickly bush." "I don't agree," murmured Ronald, his voice thick with sleep, his arse blocking our perfect view of the lake in the back garden. "Yours is the life of a natural cynic, a wastrels journey from moral cesspit to moral cesspit."

That night a burglar with an oversized torch and a vicious but toothless bulldog stole our cups, saucers, tee shirts and Ronald's ticket to Uganda. My fat friend slept through it all.
At breakfast I watched as he guzzled his coffee out of a Tupperware container, farting frequently as the previous night's spicy pizza took its revenge.
"The stink," I protested, "the stink, the stink, the stink" but Ronald wasn't listening.
"I'll have to go bare chested to the office today," he said, forcing him self into his undersized Harris Tweed jacket. "It's going to be bloody cold."
"Thank God we're insured," I snapped, "forcing myself to smile sweetly. "Maybe they'll give you the cash for that ticket of yours." "What ticket!" howled Ronald, "they didn't take my ticket to Uganda?"
Then he had a tantrum, using his massive arse to flatten almost all of my cacti, his mighty boots to kick two panels out of the kitchen door.
I was most annoyed. His nasty turns were something I definitely wouldn't miss if he departed for Africa.

Gale Treadwright's my guide in all things psychic, the person I can rely on to help me through the thickest, the jungle, the vast clump of confusion that is the after-life. She works with me on the evening shift at Barker's Filling Station, frequently sharing her knowledge of the other world with me between customers.

"Your father's standing before me holding out a bunch of spring onions," she might say.

"Fascinating," I might reply. "How do you know it's him?" "He's got your mouth and eyes."

"My mouth and eyes!" And then I'll sink into a chair and start to sob.

Father was a keen gardener who was run over by a train one wet Saturday afternoon. Mother didn't seem too concerned.

"At least he won't be bothering me for sex," was all she could say when the policeman came round. She was a hard bitch.

I felt like ripping that silly red wig of hers off and trampling it all over the front lawn.

Gale makes a splendid cup of tea, often bakes little cakes topped with pink icing and brings them into work.

"I wish you wouldn't cry so much," she said the other week after I'd broke into tears over a lost kitten, a sweet little thing that I'd found and house trained over the summer holidays.

"It makes your nose turn bright red, makes it appear far more prominent than it really is."

There are times when I think my work mate suspects I'm something less than a proper man. She's forever asking me to lift heavy boxes, eject unpleasant customers from the office, take our extremely aggressive guard dog for long walks. It annoys me but I put up with it. Her freshly baked cup cakes and psychic knowledge are things I would hate to be without.

Ronald has dreams of Uganda, insists on talking about them when I'm tired and want to nap on the settee.

"Kampala," he'll say, "Kampala and a pretty bungalow in the fading light. Palm trees, coconuts, a little woman with a devil's face selling strange puddings by the wayside. I'm there, at peace, smiling to myself while reading a John Buchan novel on a sumptuous veranda. Can you get fresh eggs there?"

I mutter something about having a hard day at the petrol pumps but he continues, fat face becoming pink and mottled with the effort of it all.

"There was a time when Rome was the place I had dreams about. Nero was my hero. Wild bears were frequently disembowelled in front of my sleeping eyes. Now it's Africa, elephants, white men in brown shirts, hairy legs, my beautiful Kampala. How do they keep their butter fresh without decent freezers? I worry about the water."

I slowly drift into a troubled sleep. Life without Ronald, if he manages to recoup the cash for his last ticket to Africa, will be a doddle. One never knows, I might be able to secure myself a loving girlfriend. This grotty little home of ours could be transformed. She might be house proud, a compulsive carpet beater and obsessive user of the feather duster. I see her now as she bends over to dust, as she shows her lacy underwear brazenly, temptingly. A brassy blonde? A shy little brunette? I really don't mind. Almost any woman will do. Nights are awfully lonely these days.

"The apex of civilization is somewhere near Walsall in Staffordshire. It's in a field near a brook near a shed made of old ice creams vans. If I'm to sit in judgement on that bamboo throne they'll provide. I'll need a red gown with an ermine collar and a pair of boots to keep the lizards away." Ronald left our shared apartment two days after he received his replacement tickets to Uganda from a surprisingly cooperative travel agent. "He was so kind," said Ronald, "offered to cover all costs until I could return the cash, said he'd deem it a great honour if I brought him a cow-hide shield and tribal head-dress back from my travels."
I was a little concerned for his sanity but kept quiet. The speech about Walsall and the boots to repel lizards stuck me as particularly odd. I often thought the size of his arse had unsettled him from an early age. Gale, who had met him in the pub a couple of times, agreed with me.
"My psychic awareness tells he could have been an extremely aggressive baboon in another life," she was heard to say after a lengthy drinking session in 'The Pirate's Lair' one night. A vision of jungles, parakeets and badly behaved monkeys wielding football rattles swept over me as I opened the car door. My raucous laughter, somehow inhuman, echoed and swirled round the empty car park.

What's my future? A cousin of mine recently offered me a job supervising his four launderettes, "filling up the soap tubs and swabbing down regularly," as he put it. I decided to turn him down. Supervising the cleansing of dirty underwear, piss stained jeans and the like is just a waste of my potential. And anyway, what's wrong with Barker's Filling Station? Where else can a man have his psychic health checked regularly? Barker's will suit me fine until I get into university. Some say I'm a little old, (I'm thirty-seven next birthday) to pass through the portals of learning but I don't think so. My brother became a Doctor of Botany at fifty-three after twenty-five years as a bus driver. There's good genes in our family. My eldest brother is living proof.

Are we really nothing? Are we really just balloons drifting in a light wind towards a prickly bush? My deep interest in the mania of others may lead me to a career in psychology. When I wake tomorrow Ronald will probably be at London airport eating a cheeseburger and fussing over his excess baggage. I might buy more cacti. I love that venomous part of their nature, the lust they have for blood when sat upon. Big Miriam could ring tonight; we could share a bowl of rice and bits of roasted pig in her smelly kitchen. "I like to cook Chinese style," is what she usually says when she offers this kind of meal. I won't argue with this. When I'm hungry there are no disputes. I'm close to the cesspit but not quite in it. A yearning for a civilized education will help keep me clear headed, relatively pure, huggable.

LIVERPOOL ARTHUR

Who is this rotund, sweating figure with his brow all Beatled, Gerry and the Pacemakered? I believe he's from the city of Liverpool, crosses the Mersey regularly and could be a walrus. "Bollocky Boo," he says in the ears of passing strangers, thus giving cause for the police to be called, dogs to be set upon him. I've counted the bites on his buttocks more times than I care to remember.

I'm his former wife. "Betty," he often says, "we were like two peas in a pod and didn't have a pot to piss in."

How right he is. Out loving innocence kept us afloat during the early years of our marriage, but now we're sunk.

His success spoilt things. If he'd never joined Peter Perkins and the Paragons we'd still be in that cosy little house of ours. Beat music destroyed his personality, turned him into a gibbering alcoholic in an ill-fitting wig, a pariah in the pub, a womaniser and cheque forger.

I can remember when he worked at the post office and only drank at weekends. I remember him changing little Bernard's diaper, smacking his bottom gently, saying something like, "Fatherhood suits me. I'm the happiest Dad in the universe."

Unfortunately my brother introduced him to the bass guitar. It was a hot summer's day at my mother's place; Eric was in the bathroom practicing. Arthur, that's my ex husband's name - I don't like it, sat listening attentively. "Could you show me a few chords," he asked my brother when he emerged.

"I think I could take to that instrument of yours. I know I've got music in me somewhere."

This was the start.

From that fateful day Arthur abandoned all rational career moves, sat himself in a corner of the living room with a bass guitar every hour God sent and practiced, practiced, practiced. Little Bernard was neglected. I was reduced to cooking meals, washing clothes and making the occasional favourable comment about his playing prowess.

The post office gave him the sack, citing persistent inefficiency and an inability to arrive on time for work as the reason. It was horror after horror until Arthur joined Peter and the Paragons and started earning money playing in pubs. The band soon acquired a following, mostly drunks who couldn't tell a symphony orchestra from a skiffle group. The noise was the thing - lots of it, and my husband, along with Peter and his obscenely loud electric guitar, definitely provided it.

Their fame grew, surprisingly, and the offer of a recording contract coupled with a nationwide tour soon followed.

It all happened so quickly and, although the sudden flood of cash provided some kind of comfort (little Bernard had the biggest sandpit and see-saw on our estate), it heralded the decline in our relationship. It was the constant touring that did it. I never knew where he was, whom he was sleeping with, what sexual diseases he was catching. Female fans wrote explicit letters from far away places, sent photos of themselves in flimsy clothing.

"Never seen her before," was all Arthur could say when I asked questions. It was a catastrophe for my ego. I felt like a lost Cinderella left out in the rain, an unattractive dancer hovering on the edge of the ballroom without a partner. I sought solace in fattening puddings, sticky cakes the size of cannon balls. Within the space of a year I turned from a sylph-like twenty-five year old into a monstrous, prematurely aged lump.

Arthur, so busy with his touring and his groupies, hardly seemed to notice. It took my mother to pull him up in his tracks. I remember the day she did it, the sound of her overflowing handbag as it crashed down on his head, his howl of pain as she kicked him in the balls.

Little Bernard joined in as well, sitting firmly on his Dad's face as he lay in a stupor.

It was a momentous event, one that culminated in the ritual burning of Arthur's bass in a fire in the back garden. The neighbours had a field day. Oh how they laughed, sneered, pointed. The collapse of our relationship was something they'd been predicting since Arthur had hit the big time. We were a tragedy waiting to happen.

Peter from the Paragons came round to see me a couple of days ago. His toothy grin cheered me up no end.

"I saw Arthur in the pub last night," he said, helping him self to a tomato from a bowl on the sideboard, munching and sucking loudly, "he had big holes in his pullover and he was pissed again."

Since the Paragons had ceased to be fashionable, Peter, having spent all his cash on several failed business ventures, had taken a job in a menswear boutique. It was a brave attempt to support his wife and four strapping young teenagers, but it wasn't working. Life had become too

expensive because the squanderous habits of a former pop star were hard to control. Peter hadn't got a clue how to manage his meagre finances, so his long-suffering wife was on the verge of leaving him.
"Did he hit anybody?" I asked, slightly irritated as Peter bit into his third tomato. "Were the police called?" the ex Paragon laughed, "No," he said, " he stole Micky Miller's bike and rode off into the night. Micky's threatening to break his legs if he catches up with him."
I thought of Arthur in his pomp: spotted bow-tie, impeccable pressed white suit, a well filled, snakeskin wallet stuffed into his inside pocket. Then I allowed my mind to drift back to a weekend in Paris, an expensive hotel room, passionate love on blue silk sheets, Arthur drunk but happier than I've ever seen him before or since. The fame and fortune was so short lived. "Daydreaming are we?" asked Peter, rising from high chair and putting a creepy arm round my waist. "Could you lend my seventy-five pounds till next weekend?" It was said in a lackadaisical, off-hand sort of way and I was immediately annoyed. "I'm broke!" I shouted, "broke, broke, broke! Little Bernard hasn't had an ice-cream for the past three weeks. I need a new bra. I'm stealing stuff from the bakery where I work to feed us both. We're in a mess. I've never been so hard up in my life."

Who is this rotund, red-faced scruffy, shouting figure wearing a belly hugging polka dot tee shirt that struggles so to climb the steep path to my front door? I believe we used to have a close relationship; that he's the father of my little Bernard, that he's just been re-released from police custody, and that he's going to ask me if he can sleep on my couch for the night. Liverpool Arthur Waddle, born on a smelly rundown housing estate, former postal worker and bassist with the late, sometimes lamented Paragons, occasional philanderer and writer of dodgy cheques.
"Are you in there my little flowerpot," he warbles through the letterbox, "have you some tea and toast for a reprobate without house or hearth?" I want to be mean and tell him to fuck off but silly, sweet memories of our past together crush my better judgement. I open the door and let him in.
"They've let me off," he says, gasping for breath; "the desk sergeant was an old fan and took pity." Tousled haired Bernard appears in the hallway gripping a roughly hewn jam sandwich.
"Want some Dad?" he asks, his little face lighting up, chubby knees filthy from an early morning romp in the back garden. Arthur, still

puffing away like a broken down steam engine, reaches out, touches his offspring tenderly on the shoulder. "Not just now son. I need a big stack of toast dripping with butter and a couple of big boiled eggs. You keep your sandwich for yourself. I bet it tastes smashing."

I walk slowly into the kitchen followed by Arthur and Bernard. My head's spinning. Where are the eggs going to come from? How can I make him a pile of toast when I've only got two slices of bread left? Why do I always take pity on him when he comes round in a state? Arthur tosses a bundle of ten pound notes on to the table. "I found this before it was lost," he says, chortling loudly, "I was down by the river yesterday and some fisherman left his wallet on top of his raincoat, right next to a goggle eyed dead carp that kept looking at me." "Some folk are very careless with their property," I say, starting to laugh, "Peter from the Paragons left his cheque book on the sideboard yesterday. He told me he's penniless but I'm not sure if he's telling the truth."

Arthur winks at me.

"We are but children of fortune," he says, "sometimes good and sometimes bad." "With cash I can buy a new bass, write some new tunes, form my own band. Peter was never a good singer, and his teeth are a joke. Have you got a letter with his signature on somewhere round the house? I think I could copy it."

"I'm off to do a bit of shopping," I say, snatching a ten-pound note from off the bundle.

"Coming Bernard?"

Bernard jumps up and down excitedly, his eyes positively glowing with joy. I decide there and then to renew my relationship with Arthur. A child's sense of security is important. Arthur could provide that.

"Will you be buying me that Easter egg you promised?" asks Bernard.

"Anything," I answer, baffled by the request, "anything."

Bernard takes my hand. It feels wonderful. Arthur puts his arms round both of us. That feels wonderful too.

Happy ending?

Don't know. Don't know at all.